Inherited Courage

Shane Massie

WestBow
P R E S S
A DIVISION OF THOMAS NELSON

WestBow Press books may be ordered through booksellers or by contacting:

WestBow Press
A Division of Thomas Nelson
1663 Liberty Drive
Bloomington, IN 47403
www.westbowpress.com
1-(866) 928-1240

Because of the dynamic nature of the Internet, any web addresses or
links contained in this book may have changed since publication and
may no longer be valid. The views expressed in this work are solely those
of the author and do not necessarily reflect the views of the publisher,
and the publisher hereby disclaims any responsibility for them.

Any people depicted in stock imagery provided by Thinkstock are models,
and such images are being used for illustrative purposes only.

Certain stock imagery © Thinkstock.

ISBN: 978-1-4497-0517-6 (sc)
ISBN: 978-1-4497-0518-3 (e)

Library of Congress Control Number: 2011921659

Printed in the United States of America

WestBow Press rev. date: 2/14/2011

I am dedicating this book to my beautiful baby girl, Kaitlyn Elaine, who means the world to me.

Contents

Chapter One

Family Heritage

And so, what is the final test of my manhood? I've asked myself that question from my childhood to the present. Do I turn and flee from the fear of my thoughts and the anticipation of the outcome, or do I dare attempt to find honor, bravery, and courage in my upbringing and in my instincts that have grown to be my life? But wait, I guess I should start from the beginning.

My name is Jack, and I have a rather reserved personality, the changes happening over the course of several years. My family is unique in every aspect of life. We are the Mayfields. Being a Mayfield seems to be a job in and of itself, except there is no monetary payment for being a Mayfield. There is, on the other hand, the reputation of the "good family" name. Sometimes, that alone could be payment enough in this old world.

My mother exceeded the average person in her love and caring for me and my sister Kate, who happened to be two years older than me. Kate radiated beauty, matched only by her smartness. It naturally made her the center of attention. I accepted this because she never asked for it to be that way. Kate had always been an over-achiever, from school academics to beauty contests, to being her own boss in a successful advertising career. I am not a "nobody" in life and society, but up against her, I always seem to take a backseat. You get used to these things, though sometimes you might think of yourself as the black sheep of the family. Nevertheless, my family is truly wonderful, from the most caring, loving mother, to the utmost number one sister, and to the man, my father, whom I've always tried to please.

My wonderful father came from a time of hardship, born during the Great Depression. His parents were common, hard-working folks who knew the value of a dollar, and whose love for the family and its welfare represented their lifetime achievements. This is where it really all begins.

My grandfather had an average stature. Of all the stories told, Grandfather Mayfield went above and beyond the measure of bravery, toughness, and what we would consider being courageous for any normal person. I still don't understand what courage is all about, so I started a long, internal search for the characteristic of courage that my grandfather and my father possessed. This inherited trait was something, I presumed, that all of the male Mayfields had. Courage made the Mayfield men tougher and braver in times of distress. The foundation of a family heritage comes from the family's stories, and the Mayfields were no exception.

The courage and bravery that my family possessed started with Grandfather Mayfield, who endured extreme hardships in life. A veteran of WW I, times of difficulty were always present. My father told me stories from when he was a boy of how Grandfather Mayfield became his role model and someone he looked up to.

The one story I do remember started when Grandfather worked as a cook in a bar and grill in Indiana in the late 1950s. He was sixty-five years old at the time, and to all the people who knew him, he was a kindly sort of man. The story goes that Grandfather Mayfield was cleaning up late one evening, and two loud and crazy drunks came inside the bar and grill, raising all kinds of hell. Grandfather Mayfield told them that in order to stay, they would have to change their "dispositions." At Grandfather's comment, the first drunk guy reached over the bar and grabbed him. Little did the guy know the uncommon toughness that all the Mayfield men possessed. They did not even see Grandfather standing next to a billy club, which happened to find its way across the back of the first assailant's head. Meanwhile, as the first guy lay unconscious on the floor, the second bad ass, who happened to be the more boisterous of the two, attempted to come around the corner of the bar to prove that the sixty-five-year-old man had met his match.

The second guy spat a stream of obscenities, expressing exactly what he would do to my grandfather once he got to him. The rest of the story goes that Grandfather Mayfield calmly picked up a skillet containing hot cooking grease from the stove, and told the second alleged bad ass man to "come and get it." This had to be an amazing sight to see a sixty-five-year-old man holding his ground against two would be tough guys.

The second guy, not being intoxicated enough, backed down, which he realized allowed him to survive. For all the stories told about Grandfather Mayfield, it is apparent that he never bluffed. There are plenty more stories of the uncommon toughness Grandfather Mayfield possessed. He appeared to be fearless.

To understand my present situation, I must continue on.

Chapter Two

Baby Steps Toward Bravery

Long ago, my sister Kate and I were in a daycare. I probably remember this because my parents worked, and daycare seemed the only answer to providing supervision. At the time, I must have been three or four years old. The daycare was run by a huge, powerful, over-bearing woman. She was overweight, which may have explained her disposition and meanness. She used to make me drink all the milk from my cereal bowl before she allowed me to have any more milk. She also did bad things to the other kids. One day, I finally stood up to this lady.

One day, she hit another kid. Even in my youth, I knew something was very wrong with this. I told her to stop hitting the other child, and that I would tell if she did not stop. My courage reigned open season, and from that point on, this woman abused me, and told my sister that if either one of us told what happened, then she would hurt me worse the next time. How is that for blackmail? It worked until the bruises showed up. Ah, those tale-tell signs.

The woman also used to take me to the bathroom and try to force food down my throat. At the same time, she would hit me vigorously across the legs and arms. I would come home with bruises all over my legs, and when my parents saw them, they confronted the lady to ask how I acquired all those bruises. She simply told them I fell down in the yard area at playtime. My sister and I never told my parents the truth, and I wished we had, because after that, I was never allowed to go outside for playtime again. The lady made sure of that. If Mom and Dad ever knew the truth, there is no doubt in my mind this lady would definitely have been the property of the state—if you know what I mean.

Not long after I came home with bruises, my parents took my sister and me out of that daycare. No doubt my parents did not feel comfortable anymore with that lady or her daycare. For years, I thought this memory represented a recurring bad dream. It just seemed so real. When I finally did ask my parents about this incident, they verified the truth of it, and that the mean old lady eventually went out of business. I suspect the other kids who were also abused finally spoke up. I have nothing but love for all children because of this incident. In my opinion, part of my childhood had been taken from me by having to experience that sort of thing. When someone abuses or neglects an innocent child, they are truly a bad person. Some children can even carry that hurt throughout their lives. Remembering this incident from time-to-time, I would wonder if that part of my life represented some kind of test.

Everyone has certain incidences in school that they wish never happened, whether it happened in elementary, junior high, or even high school. Some things were just so traumatic that they would sometimes leave a life-long impression on an individual.

One such event happened to me that became very important, that really made a difference in my life to this day. My father was a teacher at the local high school, which also had an elementary wing. Since I was only six years old at the time, I attended the elementary part. At age six, no boy likes *any* girl, much less a high school cheerleader. One day, while waiting for my father in front of the main building, a couple of cheerleaders started to flirt with me. They were doing cheers and tumbles in the grass until they noticed Mr. Mayfield's son. They stopped and taunted me about how cute I was, and said I should join their cheerleading squad as their mascot so they could see me all the time. I did what any good ole country kid at my age would do. I started throwing rocks at them.

At first, they thought me cute for throwing little rocks and all. Then I hurled this extra large rock at them. Suddenly, they stopped laughing and flirting with me, a look of disbelief covering their faces. The main high school building had two big, plate glass doors, and lucky me, I unfortunately hit one of those glass doors with the extra large rock.

The girls were shocked at what I did. No question about it, my dad was going to be really mad at me. He had already taught me right from wrong, and I knew throwing that rock was 100 percent wrong. Of course, the girls ran to find my father. I do not know if it was bravery or stupidity, but I waited for my father to come and see what I did. When he did show up, I could tell by the sound of his voice how very disappointed he was in me. He saw the damaged plate-glass door, and told me that maturity would be the one thing I would have to learn in order to go somewhere in my life. I thought six-year-old boys always threw rocks at cheerleaders who flirted with them, but really, I knew it was wrong. No doubt.

Lesson number one in life: Take control of your actions, take responsibility for your actions, then stand-up for the outcome. This particular predicament took a turn for the worse. I figured my father would either scold me, ground me, or maybe even whip me, but what he had in mind became far worse than all those other things put together. In the morning, I would have to walk into the high school principal's office and tell the principal what I did. Little did I know, my father had a close friendship with the principal and had already told him what I'd done. I felt frightened all that night, because—then and even now—in my eyes, Principal G.L. Thatcher, a huge, intimidating man with a deep voice, had a look of sheer, hard-core action. He measured probably somewhere around six feet tall, and maybe weighed 215 pounds. In my little world, he represented Goliath with at least 350 pounds of muscle. His voice boomed, commanding attention without any effort from everyone in hearing range. Nevertheless, after about thirty minutes of sleep and a night filled with tossing and turning, dawn arrived. I got up, put my clothes on, and then I had breakfast with my family.

Dad acted as though nothing was different. My mom kept looking at me with worried eyes. She knew what awaited me just hours away. She knew her baby boy would, for the first time in his little life, have to prove he had morals, goodness, and courage, and if he did not, he would always be overwhelmed by fear and setbacks in life. Meanwhile, I wrestled with the questions of what might happen, and what I should I say and do. The time came closer, and obsessive thoughts ravaged my brain. After all, I was only a kid, for goodness sakes.

My dad always took me to school, and this morning would be no different. Before arriving at the main building at the high school, he told me to be honest, tell the truth, and above all, be brave.

Finally, we reached the front office where the principal's secretary worked, and it was only a matter of time before the principal walked in. As my dad sat there waiting with me, he socialized with some of the other teachers who entered the office. I sat there and watched everything around me to relieve the stress. Suddenly, I heard that unmistakable deep voice. Turning to see, my eyes locked on Mr. G.L. Thatcher.

He looked directly at me, and his first words were, "Is there something you need to tell me, young man?"

I could barely breathe, and my boyish voice squeaked. "I broke your window," I said. The moment of truth towered over me, and I knew I was done for.

Mr. Thatcher boomed, "If you *ever* break another window at my school or misbehave in any way, you will wish you never did."

Shrinking, I said, "Yes, sir, and I am sorry."

"Okay, boy," said Dad, "wait outside for me." Wishing only to escape, I had one foot already outside the door before my father could even finish his sentence. Dad finally came outside and walked me to my class. Just outside my classroom, my dad turned to me and said, "I am very proud of you. What you just did was the right thing, and, hopefully, it will be the beginning of what it takes to be a good man— a Mayfield man."

Suddenly, I lost it. The true kid inside me came out. I tried to wipe away the tears as my father told me to go to class, and that he would see me after school.

At that moment, the incident was burned in my brain as one of those special moments between a boy and his father. I certainly learned to stand up that day.

I must say, those valuable lessons learned at such a young age do form important characteristics.

In 1974, I was a ten-year-old fifth-grader still at the same school on the Alabama coast. My father had been teaching me morals and values that represented Christian life, with an emphasis on becoming a good, honest, and tough Mayfield man who, with the right timing, should be able to take on anything the old world might throw at him. That was the idea, anyway.

Everyone knows how school can be, and we all experience and deal with the different types of kids that attend our schools. There are your typical good kids, who just want to learn and play kick-ball at recess, and then there is the school bully. This person always appears to be twice the size of most kids, probably because he failed the same grade several times. His biceps were always defined by a muscular outline, and he might even have chin hair. Chin hair on a fifth-grader should not only be intimidating to the students, but it should also intimidate the teachers. In any case, I had a bully into my homeroom. His name was Francis Terrell Smith, but he made all the kids call him Rico. He was a big kid, and he always picked on the smaller kids in the class. Our bully got in trouble every day in school. He always picked fights with everyone, and no one ever stood up to him. One could say this was a good example of the "fear factor." The "fear factor" affects a person so that they get so scared they loose control of their better judgment. They try to avoid problems instead of facing them head-on. This "fear factor" is still a mystery to me.

I would go to my homeroom class the first thing in the morning. There was one bright spot that I looked forward to each day, that made each morning very special. That bright spot was little Casey Johnson, the cutest girl in school, and especially in my homeroom class. Fortunately, she lived right down the road from me, and that, I thought, gave me a leg-up in any competition I might encounter with other fifth-grade suitors. She was the best daydream of the hour. During the entire class time, I stared at her in awe.

I used to think I could be her prince if she needed one. Little did I know that the thoughts of my adolescent heart would get the attention of the teacher. Unfortunately, it got me a seat up front by her desk because of my inattentiveness. This punishment placed me parallel to Rico, who stayed in constant trouble and therefore also had his own seat by the teacher's desk. Usually, Rico would start out sitting in the regular classroom seats, but on this one day, he "sassed" our teacher, Ms. Delk. No one ever sassed a teacher in those days. This kid was truly bad news.

As it happened, my locker stood right next to little Casey Johnson's—definitely a good thing. I always looked forward to the ringing of the bell, because I could go to my locker. Even if I did not have anything to put in my locker, I would go just to see Casey Johnson. On this particular day, I waited for the school bell to ring, and as soon as class was dismissed, I saw Rico run out the front door so he could get a good head start in making trouble for the other kids. I mean, what is the point of being a bully if you do not have ample time to pick on the other kids, right? After I gathered my books from beneath my desk, I walked outside to my locker where I could witness the cutest girl in school put her books away.

Surprise, surprise, Rico was at Casey's locker, causing her trouble. At first I acted like I did not notice anything. I proceeded to undo the combination lock on my locker when I heard Rico trying his best to work his charm on Casey. Rico proved to poor little Casey that sometimes evolution does go backward. After Casey graciously rejected Rico's advancements, he started getting ugly and called Casey some crude, unmentionable names. Seeing poor Casey in this shattered, tearful position, my judgment became clouded. Out of nowhere, I told Rico to leave her alone. Yes, those words actually came from my little ten-year-old mouth, which I suddenly realized made Rico extremely mad. *What was I thinking?* As a Mayfield, I am supposed to rise above a situation with courage and honor, but Rico had none of those qualities. After all, the guy had chin hair and probably more testosterone than me. Before I knew what happened, Rico was slamming my head into a locker. Yeah, he was really, really mad. My concern at this point became how little Casey Johnson might see me. Would she think me a coward for not fighting back? I could not let that happen.

All of a sudden, a strange feeling came over me. Not one of fear, but something I never experienced before. I was tougher than Rico and, at that very moment, I knew it. I began to kick Rico with some special cowboy boots my parents bought for me the previous Christmas. I kicked Rico with those boots, connecting with his shins on both legs. As hard and as fast as I could, I kicked and kicked Rico until Ms. Delk came into the hallway and broke it up. I say broke it up, but she really just grabbed me, because I seemed to be the only violent aggressor in this event. I struggled to get in one more kick, just to leave an exclamation mark on my own disposition. At last it was over, and reality raised its ugly head. I could not believe that I just wiped the entire hallway with Rico. Incredible personal reward came in the form of a really big smile from little Casey Johnson. The news resonated all over the school that yours truly kicked Rico's ass. Oh, how I soared! Surely, this had to be what being a Mayfield was all about. *I am a Mayfield*, I thought.

While basking in my glory, reality suddenly hit. With the rise of glory came an intense fall. I had to go home, and that meant explaining my actions to my father. The school generously assigned me to immediate detention.

Only parents could reverse detention if they chose to. That meant Father would find out. I had to face him. He not only wanted me to be a tough Mayfield man, but, on the other side, he also despised fighting and acting below good, wholesome standards. *What have I done now? Who will save me from my father's imminent disapproval and punishment?* Welcome "fear factor," that feeling I referred to earlier. Yep, now I had it.

Knowing my father would be coming down the hallway soon, I wrestled with that "fear factor" feeling. I tried to anticipate every conceivable action he might reign down on me. When he arrived at the detention room, my father opened the door, and in a very stern voice said, "Boy, are you all right?"

I replied in a very intimidated voice, "Yes, sir."

Father told me to go to the car. He did not speak the whole drive home, but as we pulled up into the driveway, he said, "If the fight was for a just cause, then I can accept that, but you have to remember that being a Mayfield is to be an honorable and courageous man, and sometimes the honorable and courageous man is the one who chooses not to fight." Go figure. I did not really understand what my father meant then, but I know now he meant that sometimes walking away is the more honorable and courageous thing to do.

Chapter Three

Caring Can Cause Courage

As a grown-up eighth grader, the "fear factor" suddenly evolves, and only that individual possesses omnipotent knowledge. In other words, hear nothing, know all. I was no exception, and I fit the stereotypical teenager. I certainly tried to understand my upbringing and accept the family tradition of being a tough and courageous Mayfield. I always seemed to miss the boat when it came to realizing what life was all about, but then again, do any of us ever truly understand all the complexities of what life is all about? I could not see myself as being as tough or honorable as the Mayfield men before me,

First my grandfather, and then my father, wore shoes of a true Mayfield man. The pressure to fill those same shoes seemed to elude me. I had asked my father on several occasions, "How will I know if I am a true Mayfield man?"

In response, he would simply tell me another story about some event Grandfather Mayfield had gotten involved in, and he would tell me how Grandfather always presented himself as a good role model in life. Little did he know that I would not be completely satisfied with just the stories. Of course, I asked my mother the same question. She pointed to my father as someone to look up to if I wanted to try and become a good man in this world. My mother would tell me a story about my father, about something he did that would portray him as an above-average, honorable, and courageous man. One particular story stands out in my mind.

During the time of school integration in the southern states, my father taught all kinds of kids for the first time, blacks and whites alike. According to the story, the night before the school integration was to start, my father received a phone call as he ate dinner with my mother and Katie. Evidently, I had not been born yet. Anyway, Dad answered the phone, and his demeanor changed after the caller introduced himself. It turned out the man calling identified himself as a member of the KKK, and he told my father that he would not be teaching those black kids the next day. As long as I have known my father, no one has ever told him what he could and could not do.

Mom told me that my father told the racist caller he had every intention of teaching school the next day. My father said that whoever showed up, no matter what their skin color, was welcome in his class. The racist caller told my father to come to the local diner, and they would make sure he did not show up for school the next day. As you could imagine, my father, being a true Mayfield man, left the house that night and went down to the diner to back-up what he believed in.

My mother was about to complete the story when my father walked into the room. I could not resist, and I asked him about the story. Modestly, he said, "Skin color does not make a person, but what's inside does." Then he left the room, and Mother continued where she left off. Shortly after the phone call, my father went to the local diner, and he drank a cup of coffee in a booth by himself. He waited for over two hours for a face-to-face meeting with the racist man who made the threat to him. Needless to say, no one ever showed up. My father came home, went to bed, and early the next morning, he arose to be the first one at school to welcome all the new kids.

Mom concluded that only a good, honorable man—a Mayfield man—would have shown so much courage. Really, though, everything my father did came naturally because of his upbringing.

It turned out Mother was right. Father and Grandfather had those wonderful traditional family traits of being good men filled with courage. In my mind, both men were good enough role models to follow. I sometimes wonder if I will ever possess the same characteristics that Father and Grandfather had more than an abundance of. Often, I refer back to my adolescence to see how different trials and tests molded my own personality. However, not all tests were tests of valor. In fact, sometimes kids just have to be kids, but even kids have their own tests to show what they might think to be signs of toughness or courage.

In the eighth grade, I had a best friend named Tim Turner. Tim was one of the toughest guys in school. His dad taught at a local boxing gym in town, and of course, Tim became his dad's prized pupil. He ended up becoming the golden gloves boxing champion for his age group. No one ever seemed to mess with my buddy, Tim. On the other hand, I always had to prove myself. It did not help one bit being Tim's best friend. Heck, he would encourage me to fight, and on some occasions would even instigate it, even though my father always taught that we should walk away, and that, indeed, I did.

The guys in the school yard knew I could be tough simply because of a game we played. We named it "Suicide," and the tough kids in the school yard invented it. The game goes like this. One kid would always bring a tennis ball to school. At break time or right after lunch, we would all go to the side of any one of the school buildings, and use the brick wall as the game area. We took a tennis ball and threw it against the wall. When it bounced off the wall, one would simply catch it and throw it back against the same wall. Sounds pretty simple, huh? Oh, I forgot to mention that if you dropped the ball when you tried to catch it from the wall, you had to run as fast as you could to touch the wall to be considered safe. As you ran toward the wall for safety, all the other kids were allowed to hit you, kick you, and basically beat you as your punishment for dropping the ball. If the ball touched you in any way without you securely catching it, you were "it." Running and touching the wall before a physical beating would become one's only sanctuary.

Only the toughest kids would play the game, and only the *very* toughest kids stood in the very back of the pack when playing game. You see, if you dropped the ball when you were in the very back, you would have to run through the entire group of fighting kids to get to the wall. Most guys at school did not play "Suicide," but every kid knew about it. Pretty soon, more and more kids were getting hurt while playing this game. There were broken noses, bruised ribs, and if you fell down before you reached the wall, heck, you might end up being out of school for a week.

It got so bad that the junior high principal outlawed the game. Any kid seen with a tennis ball, or any kid witnessed actually playing the game, was automatically suspended. I am just really glad I never ended up getting badly hurt. Still,

I am glad, even today, to be able to say that I was one of the kids who played the game.

I wonder if my grandfather ever had childhood games that only tough kids in the neighborhood would play? Father said that the only thing Grandfather ever did when he was a boy included honest, hard work. My quest would involve searching for and acquiring, through my father and grandfather, bravery, humbleness, and family courage. After all, that would be what a Mayfield was made of, and I hoped in my lifetime I would become a Mayfield man.

Chapter Four

High School Havoc

When a boy reaches the puberty years, a strange feeling comes over him as if to say, "Hey, look. I'm becoming a man." Their bodies might be telling them this, but physically looking like a man and actually portraying a man are two different things.

In high school, I remember only wanting to play sports. My dad had been an awesome ball player when growing up, and to me sports provided a temporary outlet and a way to stray from my search for family courage. I thought that playing sports would help me become a tougher and better person than normal. Sports could possibly help me grow in every aspect of my young life. Basketball became the main sport for me. To me, basketball was a very trying sport, and it dominated my life, demanding much effort and extreme physical endurance at times. Basketball did not have the protection of shoulder pads or a helmet, and yet, injuries were quite frequent. All in all, basketball helped me make friends, along with promoting good health and a good work ethic. The only problem was being labeled a "jock." To all of my high school peers, this meant that I would stereotypically want to be the center of attention, and to possess a careless disregard for teachers and school rules.

This proposed a problem, because I wanted to be a basketball player, fit in like the other "jocks," and be one of the guys. It meant breaking the rules. One rule, in particular, was to attend class. I allowed myself to be talked into skipping a class during my senior year. I knew better, but sometimes peer pressure leads us to make mistakes we might otherwise not make.

I thought skipping class would be cool, and the other kids would notice what jocks did. Oh, how wrong I was. So wrong. The people I cut class with did not play basketball and did not have the same priorities as I did. I had to convince my friends that I had to be back at school by the end of the last period class so that I could make basketball practice. I also knew my father, who still taught at the same school, would wonder where I was if I was not at basketball practice. Little did I know that as my friends and I were on our way back to the school, my dad had surprisingly showed up at my last period class to check on me. Through the hallway grape vine, he heard that I had left school. My father, being of strict and honest values, thought he would see for himself.

I got back to school, went to my class, and sure enough, I saw Dad waiting there. He asked, "Boy, where have you been?"

I told him the truth, and the next thing I knew, he turned me in to the high school principal for my punishment, which consisted of a three-day suspension. During those three days at home, I did lots of yard work to teach me right from wrong.

This was a tough lesson to learn, but, honestly, I can say that my father was trying to be a very good man who only wanted his son to walk in the same good shoes that he did. It would appear that I had to continue to learn from these juvenile mistakes in my life. I guess you could say I kind of strayed off the beaten path in high school. I went from searching for my family tradition and the inherited trait of courage to being in trouble, and basically being a jerk. *How could I ever get right with my family now?* I wondered.

I would try so hard to get back in the good graces of my father, but he would always tell me that actions speak louder than words. These words were so uncomfortable, especially after I ended up wrecking his car.

While growing up at home, I was allowed to use the family car very sparingly. I could run errands for my folks, and sometimes drive back and forth from home to school, but only on special occasions would I be allowed to use the car for my own purposes. So how did I wreck my father's car, you ask? On a Saturday afternoon, one of my friends invited me to his house to "hang out."

Okay, yes, there were supposed to be some lovely young girls that would also be hanging out, but in the end, that was irrelevant. There were no clouds on this beautiful day. I had been working in the yard all day, and as it was getting late in the afternoon, I asked my father for permission to use the car. He asked me why, and as usual, I was honest with my father. What a surprise when my father agreed to let me go to my friend's house with his car! The one stipulation was that I had to drive very slowly and be back in an hour. This sounded like a piece of cake. I got in the vehicle and proceeded to go down the road. Then it happened. An honest to goodness squirrel ran right out in front of me. Okay, I was driving a little too fast for the gravel road. As I swerved to miss the squirrel, I lost control of the car and hit an embankment.

I felt a sharp pain in my left wrist, and then I saw the steering wheel cracked by my wrist. Ouch! Not good. There were no houses around in the area, and it became obvious by the look of the radiator in the dashboard that the car was going nowhere. I got out of the car, and began to walk down the road to search for help. I fought the extreme pain in my hand while I walked. It seemed as though I had walked for miles before my friend, whom I was on the way to go see, drove by and stopped to check on me. He had seen my father's car all banged up down the road and started looking for me. When he finally found me, he saw me holding my hurt hand. I asked if he could get me to a phone to call my dad. We found a phone a ways down the road, and I called my father to tell him what had just happened. I could tell by my father's voice that he was very upset with me. The rest of the incident became a big blur, except that I remembered my father finally showed up and took me to the hospital.

He did not mention anything about the car being wrecked. His only concern was for me. This tough Mayfield man also had love, compassion, and forgiveness toward his then-bonehead son. Could this have been what it would take to get my search for the family bravery, honor, and courage back in my life?

Chapter Five

The Proper Profession

Little by little, each event that happened in my youth drew me closer to understanding and possibly attaining those special traits of the Mayfield men. At one point, though, my searching would become stagnant.

Right out of high school, I considered the military. Hey, I thought those guys were defiantly tough, brave, and courageous. After going to different military recruiters, I decided not to give up my civilian life just yet.

As the years went by, I found myself languishing at home, still living as a big kid, doing odd jobs just to make a dollar or two. What happened to striving for goals? What happened to my search? I had given up on trying to not only gain acceptance from my family, but also trying to convince myself that I deserved to represent the Mayfield family name. I had no war stories to tell of my courage or honor. I had no witnesses to any special event that could identify me as being different or above average from the next guy. I existed as a plain, normal person, and the worst part was that I was okay with that.

Then one day, out of the blue, something deep inside began calling me. I did not know what it was, but I knew it was different.

Fast-forwarding to twenty-two years old, I had recently been hired by my hometown police department. I had taken a couple of criminal justice courses here and there, and that feeling inside me that I told you about got stronger and stronger. It became clear I was meant to be a policeman. I felt led in the direction of law enforcement. From time to time, my father had expressed his desire to be a police officer. Could I possibly find my family courage in this line of work? The only way to find out would be to give it all I had. The first couple of weeks were really tough.

I often wondered what made me choose this profession; that thing behind the feeling; the direction that came from nowhere.

During my orientation, I realized that the so-called veteran police officers were all very old, though they were probably only in their late forties or early fifties. When I saw a twenty-five-year veteran, after my first night on the job, my first impression was that they looked like some kind of ancient relic. You see, I got stuck with one of those really old veterans so that I could be trained in what they called "old school" police work. In reality (and unfortunately), I would not actually be trained by these guys at all. Instead, I ended up just driving them around the city the whole night, and to top that off, I had to do every report that they were responsible for. Welcome to being a rookie. What seems funny when I think about it now is that those old-timers were not much to look at, and it became hard to imagine they had the ability to protect us.

Life is a teacher, and later on, I came to the realization that those veteran police officers had gained true honor and bravery with their many years of experience. They deserved the utmost respect from the rookies as well as people in the general public. Naturally, for a rookie patrolman, I always wanted to be in the middle of something, to be tougher, quicker, and smarter than the bad guys on the street. It appeared to me that only cops could relate to other cops at times; that they had your back no matter what. I believe that is why policemen feel connected and close to one another. Trust of a fellow officer is a factor that must be adopted in order to survive the streets. Policeman all over the world know what I am talking about. When working in public in a regular job, a person is not required to back another employee. Danger does not erupt in civilian jobs on a daily basis. Danger in police work is commonplace.

The most important lesson I learned from my training officer was that no matter what shift you worked, who you worked with, or what event took place, your main goal every day would be to return home to your family and loved ones in one piece. At times, it seemed as if no one liked the police until they needed the police. Many policemen count on their families to be there to love and support them no matter what. I guess this whole police thing is pretty personal to me, and why shouldn't it be? I have been doing this job for a very long time now.

, In my young life, I had not yet experienced the war stories that my father and grandfather experienced. Those missing stories had left me feeling like I was not a real Mayfield man, but I now had those war stories. My war stories contained action and adventure too, to say the least. I felt fortunate and thankful for every night that I would be able to go home in one piece.

Bravery and honor should go hand-in-hand with police work, along with following the law and maintaining the public's safety. Still, my whole agenda in life was to search for and find the extraordinary Mayfield bravery, toughness, and courage that my forefathers possessed. My father and grandfather lived each day with those traits. They were not a job requirement; it was just their way of life. It is as though these traits were innate to them.

How could I know what would happen one way or another? I wondered if it was possible that these traits I continuously searched for could skip a generation. If this were true, how would I explain my grandfather being the good and honorable man he naturally was? All these questions consistently passed through my mind and occupied my thoughts. I hoped that my job as a policeman could, at the very least, lead me in the right direction in my search. Then again, maybe my being a policeman was always meant to be. Perhaps I may never have been able to achieve any measure of the Mayfield traits unless I had become a policeman.

After all, my parents raised me to do right, obey rules and laws, and take up for the weak and less fortunate people in the world. Obviously, this is the job description and requirement of a policeman.

Of course, we all know that there are things in this world so evil that we need good policemen to protect us from them. At first, I wanted to be a cop for the wrong reasons—to get glory, praise, and rewards, and to ensure that I would finally be somebody. After a few years, I realized that stuff made me empty. I simply wanted to protect the innocent and right all wrong-doers in society. What happened to me, you ask? What brought about this change?

It all started with my first run-in with a real bad dude on the midnight shift I was initially assigned to as a rookie. The old-timers and I were in the briefing room getting briefed on our latest assignments and beat patrols we were responsible for, and suddenly, we heard the jailer come running down the hall screaming, "He escaped! He escaped!"

When the patrol sergeant questioned the jailer, we were told that a white male, approximately six feet four inches tall, weighing two hundred twenty pounds, with dirty-brown hair and a beard, escaped either inside or outside our jail. The dude was wanted by another agency in the state for kidnapping and aggravated assault. This meant we were dealing with a serious offender. The first instructions were from the patrol sergeant, who ordered us to secure the perimeter inside and outside the police station. Because I was a rookie, I had to tag along with my training officer. Like I said before, being a rookie was no fun at all.

The old-timers were known as veteran police officers. They always seemed to look down on all the new rookies, because we had not proven ourselves yet. The old-timers had gone through hell in their careers, and the new guys just wanted their acceptance and respect, even though they were not yet deserving of it. The old-timers hardly ever spoke to any of the new rookie cops, and would sometimes pass us in the hallways and make some sarcastic comment. Like most peons, we had to suck it up and laugh at this, and try to gain acceptance in their eyes. Nevertheless, actions speak louder than words, and only through our actions would any of the old-timers ever accept any one of the new rookies. Fortunately, this happened on rare occasions. Most rookie cops never got a chance to earn an old-timer's respect before the old-timer retired. In fact, with only a little time on the force, how could any of us ever compare to the twenty or thirty-year veteran?

Anyway, as I followed my training officer around like a lost puppy, he told me that we were going to look inside the department to see if the bad dude could still be around. The jailer told us before we left the briefing room that the bad dude escaped through a ceiling tile in the roof of the police station. This meant the criminal would have to crawl on support beams to get to an exit. Nothing supported the ceiling tile itself. As my training officer and I policed the station, we heard a noise in the police lounge where all the policemen and women took their breaks and socialized. We both looked at each other at the same time, and then we heard it again.

Suddenly, five other senior police came to where my training officer and I were standing and said, "He's up in the roof. He hasn't left the building, yet."

Okay, I thought. *What's next?*

The patrol sergeant came to where we were all standing and said, "Somebody needs to go up in the ceiling and get him." The whole lounge got very silent. None of the old-timers wanted to go crawling around in the ceiling with this escaped bad dude who was desperate to do whatever to get free. Most of these veterans were fixing to retire, and they had already proven their valor and courage on more than one occasion in their careers. They certainly did not want to take a chance on getting hurt under these circumstances so close to retirement. You could really sense what all the old-timers were thinking. They certainly hoped someone else would volunteer.

It was my big chance. After all, I was a cocky, rookie cop destined to look fear and danger in the face. I wanted the adventure and excitement, so I spoke and said, "I'll go up."

Just then, for the first time, the old-timers acknowledged my existence. They looked at me differently, and they asked me if I needed anything. I told them I had not been issued a flashlight yet, and the next thing I knew, a bunch of flashlights were offered to me. They spoke to me as if I were their pupil, encouraging me to take over the situation. They gave a great deal of advice and a strong boosting to my confidence. It was great! I finally felt like one of the guys, something I had not been successful at when I was in school. Later, I realized that what I did gave each old-timer a gracious way out; that they could still keep face and maintain their honor, bravery, and, yes, their courage intact.

Ready to rock 'n' roll, I stepped onto a table and climbed up into the ceiling. I thought, *What am I doing?* Obviously, there was no thinking at all on my part. This was a really bad dude, and I had no weapon except for a flashlight and a can of pepper spray used by officers to spray in the eyes of suspects to try and subdue them. I had to leave my gun on the orders of the patrol sergeant, who stated it was not safe to have the gun up there while trying to get the escapee. He believed that the bad dude might have the chance to get the gun away from me. After all, as a rookie policeman, I had not yet been trained to do certain things.

Whether or not they even offered training on what I was fixing to do would be a question for later. Armed with pepper spray and a borrowed flashlight, I prepared to pull the escaped criminal down from the ceiling. Little did I know that the spot where I went up into the ceiling was only a few feet from where the bad dude hid. I turned the flashlight on him, and could see him lying very still with his face away from me. He was playing possum, I guessed.

In a firm voice, I said, "Let me see your hands." He acted dumb. The guys below were worried about me and kept calling my name to let me know they were right there underneath me. Suddenly, the bad dude started to crawl in the opposite direction. I knew he could get away if he made it to the other end of the rafter beam, which was located right next to an open exit. I pursued the escaped criminal on this very narrow support beam with only several blocks of ceiling tile to separate us.

Suddenly, the suspect stopped, changed direction, and came right at me. My senses heightened. The Mayfield blood kicked in. I felt scared at this point. The bad dude, desperate and determined to succeed, was ready to escape no matter what. It was either him or me.

The next thing I knew, he grabbed for me, and I tried not to fall from the rafter beam. As he threw his arm toward me, I let him have it with the pepper spray. I must have emptied half the can on him. The only thing I remember during the whole ordeal was that I lost my footing and started to fall right through the ceiling tile. On my way down, I did what any twenty- or thirty-year veteran would do—I grabbed the bad dude's leg and took him with me. Yep, we both fell right through the ceiling tile and onto the hard police station floor.

The next thing I remember, the old-timers came up to me to make sure I was not hurt. At the same time, some of them grabbed the so-called bad dude, escorting him politely into a "lockdown" jail cell where he was cuffed to all four corners of his bed.

I did not really realize what I had done until the next day. Everybody started talking to me and making sure I was okay. The patrol sergeant told me "good job," and all the old-timers told me I could ride with them any time. What a prestigious offer! The ceiling tile had a big hole in it for at least a week, maybe to show the first adventurous confrontation I had come against in the profession as a police officer. No matter what everyone else thought about my little moment of valor, I still had doubts. I kept thinking what happened up in the roof of the police station was pure, blind luck. I was not sure if I was brave and courageous like some of my peers might have perceived me. Had I finally found my supposedly inherited courage?

This question haunted my every breathing minute. I wanted so much to tell my dad the story of how I prevailed against a bad guy in the ceiling of the station, but even if I did get a chance to tell him, it could not equal his and Grandfather Mayfield's stories of honor, bravery, and courage. What was next for me? Where should I look? How will I know if I am deserving of the Mayfield name? Did the family name alone mean I already had courage? If so, why did I doubt myself? Why did I continue to search for this family trait that I felt would grant me manhood and acceptance as a Mayfield man in my family's eyes and in society?

As the time passed, days became months, and I remained a rookie cop, no matter how one looked at it. An example of my juvenile, rookie inexperience came when I least expected it. It all started as I was fixing to complete my training.

Chapter Six

Out for Lunch

When rookie police officers were in so-called training, they basically had to do whatever their training officer told them to do. That meant wherever the training officer wanted you to go, that's where you went. Whenever the training officer wanted to take a break, you did also, and so on. It also meant that wherever your training officer wanted to eat, you guessed it, you ate there, too. This was just part of being a rookie, and even after my first run-in with what might be called courage, things remained the same, no exceptions. The only difference was that I had a training officer who now had a little respect for me. After all, he worked the night I went up in the ceiling to get that bad guy, so he had a little more patience and understanding for me, even though I was still a rookie. My training officer was John Luner, and he was a twenty-year veteran on the force. After riding with him for six months, he finally allowed me to start calling him John instead of Training Officer Luner. This must have been a gesture of respect, since all the other rookie cops were still being treated with the "old school" mentality by the veteran police officers.

I was almost finished with my so-called training on the night shift, and after a few loops through the city, John said, "It's time to get something to eat."

I said, "It sure is. I am starving," thinking we were going to a restaurant to get something to eat.

My partner said, "Jack, I think I'm going to go back to the police station and eat my dinner there." Now I was forced to watch my training officer eat his own dinner, brought from his home, while I went starving. John surprised me by saying, "If you want, take the squad car by yourself and get you something to eat. Just be sure not to answer any calls, or make any other stops."

I said, "Sounds great."

John emphasized, "Go straight to a restaurant and come right back."

At that moment, I thought I had it made. It felt like I was finally on my own, and that was awesome. Realistically, though, I was still not on my own. I got the keys from John and went to the squad car sporting a huge smile on my face.

Late at night, there were few restaurants to choose from. I decided on The Curb, probably so named because it sat on the curb of a very busy intersection, to get me some breakfast.

On my way to The Curb, the police radio held my attention. I remembered what John just got through telling me. Do not stop anywhere else. Go right there and come right back, and most importantly, do not answer any calls. I have to admit it was pretty tempting to maybe assist when I heard all the calls belching out over the police radio, After all, I was a policeman. Rookie or not, my job warranted me to protect and serve.

Finally, I arrived at The Curb restaurant to get a nice, peaceful meal. When I turned into the parking lot, I noticed something very strange. There was a black man lying hurt in the middle of the parking lot. A blue Dodge's driver's side door appeared wide open with no one in it. It drove out of control in a continuous circle in the restaurant parking lot. The car moved pretty fast, spinning more and more out of control, causing it to make even wider circles. Suddenly, the car hit an electric pole, which temporarily caused it to slow down before it began to speed up again and continued to spin in circles. Just about every turn, it would slam into the electric pole and slow down just for a moment before gaining its momentum back. This went on in front of me a few times, and finally I realized, "Hey! I'm the police." It was my job to know what to do. I called over the police radio to my training officer, John, and told him what was going on.

He said, "Don't do anything; I'm on my way."

This was easy for him to say. A crowd was collecting, and everyone inside the restaurant came outside to watch this unbelievable event.

I had to admit, a car driving in circle by itself definitely classified as unusual. The hurt guy, who had lain in the parking lot, crawled to the sidewalk where the other people were standing. The car spun more out of control going faster and faster. There was incredulous laughter and pointing from the crowd.

The dilemma: No driver inside, and no way to stop it. There had been no training for this situation, and I wondered just how my training officer would handle it when he finally did arrive. All I could do at that moment was insure the safety of the crowd standing by. As I was thinking about what to do, the car suddenly hit the electric pole again, and this time the electric pole started to lean. Things were looking more dangerous now. The vehicle slowed down a little bit and then began gathering momentum once again, continuing in a so-call "doughnut" movement in The Club's parking lot.

It hit the electric pole again, and wow! Sparks flew as the electric pole started leaning even more. It was obvious that just a few more hits to the pole would bring it down, exposing live wires to the crowd.

Now, I thought, *we have a big problem!* If the electric pole fell, innocent people could get hurt, possibly by a traveling current if someone was standing by it. What could I do right at that moment?

Think Jack, think Jack, I kept telling myself. John had not shown up yet. I felt it was time to think on my feet, and quickly. There was no time to wait for John. I assessed the situation. I could try and jump past the open car door to the driver's seat and put on the brakes, even though I did not know why the car was doing circling in the first place. The only problem with my plan would be picking the best time to jump on board. At what point and time could I do that? It was risky for sure.

I continued to watch the spinning car as I tried to figure out when to make my move, which had to be way before the car hit the pole again, or just after it hit the pole and slowed down. It became all about timing, because I did not know what was wrong with the car to begin with, how it started on its own doing what it was doing, and whether the brakes would work once I got inside.

Another dilemma that loomed in the back of my mind was disobeying my training officer and taking matters into my own hands. This, too, became a tough decision due to it being so early in my career. John had given me a direct order not to do anything until he got there. I did not believe anyone could imagine this situation, even my training officer.

To gain some courage, I needed to remind myself about being a Mayfield. Those supposed inherited traits in my blood; bravery, courage, and good ole fashion guts. Looking back, maybe being a little crazy could possibly have been there as well. Nevertheless, I watched the car hit the electric pole for the last time. It was time to prevail over the situation.

As the car slowed again after hitting the electrical pole, I took a running start and dove through the open driver's side door and into the car seat. I tried to get my bearings, shocked that I actually made it, and just in time, but the electric pole was quickly approaching, and oh, my goodness, this looked bad.

I sat up in the driver's seat quickly and slammed on the brakes, stopping the car just before it hit the leaning electric pole once again. Sparks and bright flashes continued to spew as I turned off the car.

I immediately exited the vehicle and went over to the sidewalk where the spectators had witnessed my crazy feat.

I checked on the hurt man who assured me he was all right, but I called an ambulance for him just to be on the safe side. Later, we found out the vehicle needed to be jump-started. It turned out that the vehicle ran over the man, and he got out of the way as the car continued to circle out of control in the parking lot until I stopped it.

Gathering information for a police report, my training officer, John, showed up and checked on me. I told him what had happened. Scratching his head, he kind of smiled at me and said, "You really jumped into that moving car?"

I said, "I had to, or someone could have gotten hurt really badly."

John said, "Come on, let's go back to the police station and finish the report."

I asked him if it would be okay for me to get a bite to eat from the restaurant.

John jokingly said, "As long as you don't get into anything else."

I knew John was kidding with me, and I had to admit, it was pretty funny to be in that predicament. Anyway, I did not give it much more thought as I ordered me some late night breakfast.

As I awaited my order, I heard back from the emergency medical people who had looked after the injured man, and they told me he would be okay. He was a little banged up, and he sustained some bruises, but he would live another day. Hopefully, maybe he would not have to ever jump-start another vehicle again.

Finally, my order came, and as I poured syrup on my two fluffy, buttermilk hot cakes, two older gentlemen approached my table. They introduced themselves to me and asked, "Are you that young police fellow who jumped into that moving car?"

I said, "Yeah, that was me."

They said they were retired Alabama state troopers, and one said, "Son, I never seen anything like that in my twenty-five years of law enforcement."

I remember it well, because I said to them, "Please don't tell me that, because I have only been a cop for six months." We all laughed. After they left, I finished my meal. As I sat there, I wondered if those troopers maybe were a little impressed with what I had just done. Then I thought, *Naw, that doesn't seem likely,* but maybe, just maybe, they had noticed something different about me.

Had the search that drove me from my youth— that deep, passionate search for the family traits—finally come to the surface? Had I been brave? Had I showed signs of honor, and most of all, courage? Could this situation have finally made me deserving of the Mayfield name?

These questions circled in my brain for the rest of the night, and to my dismay, I still felt unsure of the answers. The uncertainty became the barrier that kept me from professing my right to be a Mayfield. What I had just done could have fallen under the guidelines of a normal, job-related duty; a typical requirement of a police officer. I mean, police officers all across the world are supposed to protect and serve, and since I never received a commendation by the department for my role in the car incident, it must have been regarded simply as an average situation that a normal policeman resolved.

For now, I would have to go back to the drawing board, wondering where I should look to answer those questions about honor, bravery, and courage. Who would reassure me? How would I know when those important family traits showed themselves? What would distinguish me from others? More importantly, would I ever find a balance in my life without knowing if I was truly a Mayfield man? When would the most important family traits show up that would definitely separate me from all other men? Where were those traits that my father had, and his father before him? Where or when would my inherited courage be revealed?

Chapter Seven

Nightmare in Narcotics

I have been on the force for a few years now. As a rookie policeman, I had grown into a semi-professional lawman. Still, I was somewhat "green" with some aspects of law enforcement, although I had become a lot more aggressive when arresting bad guys and in performing my everyday duties. I started to settle in and feel comfortable with daily routines as a police officer.

One day, I got an official police letter from the Chief of Police. It stated: Officer Mayfield, report to the Narcotics Division on the first of November. *Oh, no*, I thought. *What have I done now?* I thought about when I fell through the roof of the police station, and, oh yeah, let's not forget about that crazy stunt of jumping into an out-of-control car. Maybe the Chief thought I could be a liability, and by sending me to the Narcotics Division, no one would have to worry about me. This was the only thing I could think of, because I never put in a transfer to the division on my own.

I thought, *What the hell? I will make a couple of drug arrests and make everyone happy, and maybe I'll get reassigned back to my good ole patrol division within a few weeks.*

Upon reporting to the Narcotics Division, I was told that I just so happened to look very young and unlike a cop, that they could best use me to do what we called "undercover work." That meant portraying myself as a drug user or a really bad guy by trying buy illegal drugs from the *really* bad guys. This sounded bad to me.

Who knows though, maybe this could be the route to take in life that would help lead me to find the courage inside myself associated with the Mayfield name. I became willing at that point to give it a chance. But let us face it: Me, an undercover cop? I mean, could I act like a bad guy, or, much less, a drug user?

The big thing about buying illegal narcotics while in an undercover capacity was that one usually went with a semi-bad person called a Confidential Informant, or a CI. Most CIs were semi-bad people, because they were either working off their own drug offense to get a lesser one, or they were after money that most police departments gave for information about drug-related issues. These CIs varied from all races and sexes, to people who just had nowhere else to go.

In my very first undercover narcotics assignment, they sent me to a rural location in the county with a white female named Cindy. Cindy, a former drug junkie, had been caught buying and using drugs, so in order to get a lenient sentence, she had to help get an undercover policeman, who turned out to be me, into a drug circle in which I would be able to buy drugs from some major drug dealers. Contrary to popular belief, it was not simple to just go anywhere and buy any kind of drug. Most drug dealers only sold to people they knew, and they could pick out a cop when they saw one. You could say I had my work cut out for me.

Cindy's big job, basically, would be introducing me to the drug dealers she knew, and then let me do the rest. Going with Cindy gave me some credibility and insurance. The drug dealer would already know Cindy used drugs, and they would naturally assume that I used too, providing they did not catch on that I was a cop. The bad thing about doing undercover work? No backup. That meant no police officers would be close by to help if needed. Not a good situation at all.

However, we had what they called a surveillance team. These guys usually rode around in a car listening to a body wire the undercover cop wore. They could not get too close to where you actually were, because they might blow your cover. Still, a surveillance team was better than nothing at all.

We asked, "Cindy, who is our contact?"

She said, "It's this guy named Scooby."

"Is he dangerous or not?"

"Well," she said, "he's been known to have a temper, and he does carry a gun." This was not a comfortable feeling. She continued, "Scooby is a really big-time dealer of crystal meth, and he only sells to people he knows."

Our consensus was that this guy sounded dangerous, and could be more trouble than he was worth.

Cindy said, "As long as you're with me, you'll be fine."

Boy! How reassuring could that be? Imagine putting your trust in a former drug user to help get you through a sticky situation.

"You need to start out slow with Scooby," she said. "You should only try to buy some marijuana from him at first."

"Whatever you say," I said.

As we rode down the rural, dirt county road, I started talking to my surveillance team through the body wire. I usually wore my body wire in the small of my back, but the surveillance team could not talk back to me this way. They could hear everything I said, but I could not hear their reply.

I said to my surveillance team, "I have this really bad feeling in the pit of my stomach, and I really don't feel good about this Scooby character."

"Understand, buddy," came the reply. I knew being a team player had to be more important than my gut feeling. Perhaps if I pulled in the Mayfield blood, it might help get me through this trying time.

As we approached the driveway to Scooby's house, I remember seeing this older model white van sitting in the yard with all four tires flat. This played a very important part for my life in the days to come.

Cindy and I got out of the vehicle and went to the front door, and she rang the doorbell. The door opened, and there stood a white male who looked to be somewhere in his late forties. His clothes were wrinkled, and he wore thick-looking glasses. The only other characteristic that stood out was a vertical scar down the side of his forehead, no doubt received from a bad barroom experience or another confrontation.

The man started talking with Cindy, and then she introduced me. "Meet my cousin, Frank, from Georgia." Frank became my undercover name. Cindy said, "Scooby, Frank will be staying with me in town for a few days, and we wanted to get high." She tried to convince Scooby that I was a drug user and needed some hook-ups while I was in the area.

Scooby cased me with a puzzled eye, but since I was with Cindy, he seemed to dismiss the idea that I may be a cop. Scooby was a bit standoffish to me and asked Cindy, "What kind of hook-up you looking for?"

"We just need a little weed to get by with for tonight."

Weed was what we used to call marijuana in narcotics. Scooby said, "Y'all come follow me to the bedroom."

As we walked down a narrow hallway that approached his bedroom, I started to notice something really strange. I heard a kind of screeching noise. It sounded like a radio with a broken frequency. Cindy and I were only a few feet behind Scooby when he first entered his bedroom, but the strange noise kept sounding like it was getting closer.

How very odd that no one else reacted to the strange noise. No doubt it came from Scooby's bedroom. He entered first, then me, and finally Cindy.

It was obvious now that the broken radio frequency sound was coming from the bedroom. My body wire that was supposed to record my conversation with Scooby was affected by the radio frequency. Panic set in.

I thought to myself, *Jack, you've got to act fast.* The only thing I could think to do was switch off the body wire without Scooby seeing me do it. As soon as Scooby turned away from me, I reached under my shirt and turned the body wire off.

The sound finally stopped. I hoped Scooby did not put two and two together. *Did Scooby know what was happening? Does he now know I am an undercover cop?* These questions popped up in my mind, not to mention the realization that I did not know what to expect next. My heart pounded in my chest, and blood ran cold through my veins.

Scooby surprised me. He did not change his demeanor one bit. He simply asked, "How much weed do y'all want?"

Obviously, he had not caught on. Surely he could not be one of those really uneducated rednecks I had heard about, could he?

"We need at least a half ounce," I said.

This was a small amount by some standards, but the game plan was to just get any illegal narcotic I could this time, and later we would go for the big score. After Scooby reached under his bed and brought out an off-blue color suitcase, I knew we were fixing to get the hook-up.

"Do you have the money?" Scooby asked.

"How much?" I asked.

"A half ounce will cost you $200."

I counted out the money and gave it to Scooby, and in return he handed me a clear plastic baggy containing what looked like marijuana. Feeling uncomfortable, Cindy and I wasted no time in getting the *hell* out of there.

As we drove away, I said, "It's real strange that Scooby never asked me any questions about myself." I mean, here we had a big time drug dealer who was supposedly leery of the police, but instead, he had a not-to-worry attitude. I expected him to ask me every question in the book, but he asked nothing. Then when I heard my body wire cause interference with his police scanner, I was sure he would be suspicious of my identity, and, if nothing else, search me. Still, nothing happened. Maybe he was just plain dumb, or maybe, just maybe, I was just plain lucky.

After Cindy and I got back to the police station, my surveillance team came up to me to tell me I did a good job. They also told me that they could hear my body wire over Scooby's police scanner. This did not sound right to me, because more likely than not, Scooby did know something was going on.

"I guess I won't be buying any more illegal drugs from him," I said. Surprisingly, the surveillance team did not smile when I made that comment.

Then one of them said, "Jack, we need you to try and make at least one more buy from him." You see, the more times you buy from a bad-guy drug dealer, the better the chance of getting him convicted and sentenced to a long stay in our nice prison facility.

I contemplated not doing another drug deal with Scooby again, but the old Mayfield thing pierced my mind again. A Mayfield man should be more than average in toughness, but still, did I possess the courage needed to get me through this? I did not know what to do. Lucky for me, I had the weekend off to sit back and just relax.

During the weekend, I visited with my family. I told them I was going through some tough times in the department, and I remember my father telling me, "A true man has complete control over all his emotions."

"What do you mean exactly?" I said.

"It's something you have to figure out on your own," he said.

Damn, there goes my father's tough love for me.

As the weekend wound down, I got a call from the police department. It was Captain Span, head of the Narcotics Division. Captain Span said, "I heard you did a good job last week buying weed from Scooby. You know, the Narcotics Division has been after Scooby for years." Then he asked, "Would you consider attempting to buy some more illegal drugs from Scooby? Jack, we really need you to help us out on this one, if you can just hang tough for one more buy. Scooby really needs to go down, and without your help, it might be impossible for that to happen."

I did not know what to say. My back was up against the wall. The first time I lucked out buying marijuana from

Scooby, and now I was sure he knew I was a cop. I told Captain Span, "I really want to help, but I think my safety might be an issue because of the frequency interference with the scanner. Scooby had to wonder."

Captain Span said, "Jack, don't worry. We'll have a surveillance team real close this time, and we'll set up the deal to take place somewhere in the city. How's that sound?"

It did not sound reassuring to me.

Captain Span continued, "Just be brave this one time, and have courage."

Bingo. After hearing that, I absolutely knew I had to do it. I said, "You can count on me, sir." That was the call for the Mayfield man.

I hung up the phone and wondered how long it would be before I was called upon to actually go out and do this deal with Scooby.

On Monday, I still had not gotten a call yet from my surveillance team to do the drug deal. As the afternoon drifted into the late evening, I finally got the call from Jake, head of the surveillance team. He said, "Jack, we got it all set up. Meet us downtown at the back of the warehouse in thirty minutes."

"Okay," I said and hung up the phone and began to get my gear together. The warehouse was just that—an old abandoned warehouse. It was used to store paper products. Thirty-minutes was not a lot of time to prepare for a major drug deal. I mean, I did not even know what illegal drug I was supposed to be buying yet. Finally, I got everything together and headed over to the warehouse. I looked at my watch. It was 9:30 p.m. I really hated doing these kinds of deals at night, but that was the time most drug dealers did all their big business.

Upon arriving at the warehouse, Jake greeted me and said, "Here's the plan. Go to the local convenience store down the road called the Stop n' Shop. In the parking lot there, wait along side of good ole Cindy. Scooby's supposed to come and sell you ten ounces of marijuana." This was a lot of marijuana. I mean, this was considered a really big drug deal.

"How did this all get set up with Scooby?" I asked Jake.

"Cindy helped set everything up on our request and guidance," he said. "She told Scooby you were leaving to go back to Georgia, and you wanted some weed to take back and sell."

"Come on," I said, "Scooby won't believe that. He probably thinks I'm a cop already."

Jake replied, "Jack, just trust us. We've taken care of everything."

Now, when someone tells you to *trust them* in this profession, the only real advice to give is *trust nobody*. Go with your own instincts, and see what hand you are dealt.

I was still at the warehouse when Cindy pulled up. The surveillance team got me a new body wire. They tried to reassure me that the deal was safe. After my body wire was in place, Cindy and I got into a confiscated car and proceeded to the Stop n' Shop. When we arrived at the parking lot of the Stop n' Shop, we pulled up along side a payphone. Cindy said she would call Scooby and tell him we were waiting on him. After Cindy used the payphone, I spoke into my body wire the number to the payphone, and asked my surveillance team to call that number. Inside, I questioned this particular drug deal that I had very bad feelings about.

After I got off the phone with the surveillance team, Cindy and I stood by the payphone that was just off the side of the store itself. We waited for about five minutes. Just then, an old, ragged-looking late-'80s model white van started to pull into the parking lot.

It was Scooby in the same white van I saw earlier last week in his yard with four flat tires. At first, I did not know what to make of it, but then Cindy said, "Why is he in that van? He never drives that van."

My nerves edged as the hair on the back of my neck stood straight up. "What do you mean, he never drives that van?"

"Well, he has three other vehicles to use, and I never saw him use that van before. It has always been broken down in his yard," she said.

There went that "gut feeling" telling me something was wrong.

I watched Scooby drive up to the front of the convenience store and go inside. We were about fifty feet from the van, and I saw Scooby make eye contact with both of us, so he knew we were there. For some strange reason, I got fixated on the van, and could swear I saw the curtain on the back window move.

I spoke into my body wire, telling my surveillance team that someone seemed to be hiding in the back of the van. At this point, fear rose in me. I tried so hard to focus on being a Mayfield. I told myself I could do this, and that I should try to hang tough.

Strangely, Scooby remained inside the convenience store. It had been over five minutes now, and for someone who was fixing to make a lot of money off a large supply of marijuana, it did not seem right he would procrastinate inside the store. What could he possibly be doing in there for so long?

Then it came to me. Some convenience stores have police scanners in them, and maybe this one did, too. Maybe, he could be checking to hear any interference on a police scanner in the store. Now, *that* made sense.

I quickly informed my surveillance team of my theory, however, they were not able to talk back to me unless they called the payphone I stood right next to.

Then it happened. Scooby came outside the store, got into his van, and drove right up to where Cindy and I were standing. I approached the van cautiously, and Scooby stayed seated in the driver's seat.

I talked first and said, "Hey, do you got the stuff, man?"

"No, man, we have to go get it," Scooby said. "Come, jump in the van, and we'll go get it." First rule of doing undercover work is never let the suspected violator call any of the shots or change the initial game plan.

"Well," I said. "I can't leave the payphone because I'm expecting a phone call from someone."

"Come on, man, it's right down the road," he said.

"No," I said, "I have to wait on my phone call."

Just then the payphone began ringing. It knew my surveillance team was calling. They had been listening to everything over the body wire. I picked up the phone to hear Jake tell me, "Jack, get the hell out of there! It sounds like a hit. Act like you're talking to someone else."

I just said over the phone, "yes"; "yeah"; "Uh-huh."

There was a chance Scooby bought into it, and when I finally got off the phone, I told Scooby, "Man, I got to go. My friend is waiting on me, and I have to take Cindy back home before I go and get him."

Scooby looked puzzled and said, "Well, I guess we can't do business then."

"Not this time, anyways." I said.

Then Scooby drove off in that raggedy white van, and I felt like this huge rock had been lifted off my shoulder.

Just out of curiosity, I walked into the convenience store to see if my hunch was right. Guess what? Right behind the cashier's drawer, next to the register, stood a new police scanner. Sometimes it was hard to be right.

As I left the store, Cindy and I drove back to the warehouse where we met up with my surveillance team. I took my body wire off and Jake told me, "Jack, I really felt like they were going to take you away in the van and try and take you out."

"No, you think?" I said with a very sarcastic attitude. Let's face it, I was still pretty upset about the whole thing. It was not everyday one would think somebody was going to actually try and kill them. I was now certain of my theory that Scooby definitely thought I was a cop.

After Cindy left, the surveillance team tried to make me feel like I was a part of their family. I knew inside that narcotics was not for me. As a policeman involved in the Narcotics Department, you could get who you were mixed up with what exactly you hoped to accomplish. It would become your life against some drug dealer who could care less whether you made it home or not.

Driving home that night, I pondered several thoughts and feelings. Could this profession be what I wanted to do? Would I find my family trait supposedly bred into me? Courage, could it be out of my reach? Am I just a plain, normal, simple guy? Why has the search been so important to me? I almost got killed over some marijuana. Did what I had done show any signs of courage or bravery? In my own eyes and heart, the answer still remained, "No."

Chapter Eight

Cold "SMASH"

After my short but adventurous career in narcotics, I put in a transfer request to return to patrol. I missed riding around in the old black and white squad cars, and I missed going door-to-door helping persons who could not take care of their own problems. I say "own problems" sarcastically, because have you ever stopped and wondered, if policemen help everyone else with their problems, then who helps the policemen? A good question, huh? That has yet to be answered. More than likely, I think that policemen have to depend on their own families to help them.

Most policemen I know have very strong family ties. This, I think, may be why I want so very much to have my family's acceptance; to be an honorable and courageous Mayfield man. Whatever the reason, I knew that going back to patrol would not keep me from searching for my family heritage traits. I would search and search, until I was either able to determine if I was deserving of the name of Mayfield, or if I, too, possessed the one characteristic that all men—not just Mayfield men—want, and that would be courage. Otherwise, I would search until, at long last, I came to realize I may be just a very plain, normal guy who could not measure up to his father and grandfather before him.

One day, I received a phone call from the patrol sergeant on the midnight shift. That was the shift I previously worked and left in good standing. The patrol sergeant advised me that the request for my transfer back to patrol had been accepted, and that I was to start working that night from 11:00 p.m. 'till the end of the shift at 7:00 a.m.

I was so excited. Finally, I was out of narcotics and doing what I missed doing. Still, patrol work could be just as dangerous, although many of the people we dealt with were not as dangerous as the big bad drug dealers who always had their own protection. I mean, all patrolmen have to wear bulletproof vests just to be able to work the streets. I did not mind, though, knowing that one day that bulletproof vest could save my life.

Upon my return to the midnight shift, I nervously wondered how the other officers were going to act toward me. I wondered if, at this point, I would still be looked upon as a rookie in the eyes of the old-timers.

I had a few years of law enforcement under my belt now, and I had even done a tour of duty in narcotics. Believe me, nobody ever wants to work narcotics. No matter what everybody might have thought of me, I still had a unique reputation that had followed me around since the start of my career. I was known as a crazy cop who would do just about anything. My fellow officers heard all about how I fell through the ceiling of the police station, and how I "dove into" an out-of-control moving car with no one in it. They might have even heard of my more discreet narcotic actions that, unfortunately, I could not share due to confidentiality. Jack Mayfield was a crazy cop who might even be considered a rebel to some extent. I just hoped that no matter what the rumors were, or what reputation I had, I would always be known as a good cop who cared about others. Nevertheless, things remained the same.

Would you believe that some people always seem to have "trouble" follow them. I happen to be one of those people.

I had been assigned my own squad car, and I was to patrol the very southeast corner of the city, so south that I could sneak across into the next county if I wanted. Well, anyways, I started doing my normal patrol routines, checking on store clerks, checking locked up businesses, and answering any calls that dispatch gave out in my territory. It seemed to be a very slow night, and I guessed that maybe this could be normal. One hour went by, then another. When a shift turned out this slow, it could be really hard to stay awake. 11:00 p.m. until 7:00 a.m. could be a lonely shift to work without a partner to help keep you awake.

This night seemed harder than normal because it was so cold, temperatures falling to a record low for that area. I was not only alone in the squad car with my thoughts to entertain me, but I also had to use the car heater, which made me real sleepy. The clock slowly ticked by, and I remembered that not long from now, I would already be getting off work.

At 5:30 in the morning, I could not wait to go home and fall asleep in my own warm bed. The night had been so slow and quiet, and there had been complete radio silence from our dispatch. Dispatch directs emergency calls to all patrolmen, firemen, and ambulance services. It seemed as though no one needed help that night. Just as I got relaxed in my squad car and thought about what I was going to order for breakfast, a loud female voice came over the police radio. By the tone in her voice, she seemed excited, and she said, "All units, all units, be advised a car accident has just occurred. The vehicle is upside down in the nearby Quail Lake."

Quail Lake was a local lake where many people liked to fish. The lake itself stood in the county, but it was also close to the city. The local police could probably respond faster than any county deputy.

Guess whose territory it came closest to? Yeah! You guessed it. I notified dispatch that I would be en route to assist with the accident, and I sped off with all my lights and sirens going.

I listened to the police radio to see where my closest backup unit would be, and the dispatcher came back over the radio saying, "All units, all units, be advised the car still has people in it."

Not good news. I had fished at this lake before, and I knew it to be really deep in some places, not to mention the temperature of the water was so cold. Just the thought of getting wet made me think of catching pneumonia or something else. The lake was in a wooded area away from any main streets, so I knew that once I got out there, my hand-held police radio might not work. As I neared the lake, I let dispatch know. As I approached the lake, I turned off the blue lights and siren. Two white females and one white male stood on the bank of the lake, yelling down toward the water.

When I got to where they were standing, I asked them if they were all right. One of the females said, "We were not in the car. It is still in the lake, and people are trapped in it."

Obviously, this meant some nearby neighbors had now become spectators. Oh, how the police love nosey spectators. I asked them, "How many people have you seen in the car?" I should have asked first how they knew people were in the car. The two females screamed in shock, and the male did all he could to keep them under control.

Ignoring the females and the male, I had to see if I could tell where the car actually went into the lake. It was still dark from the early morning hour, and with a haze from the cold air, it was extremely difficult to see the deep, dark lake. Looking up and down the bank of the lake, I finally discovered tread marks where the car entered the lake. Now I had some idea of where the car might be. Suddenly, the haze broke for just a moment, and I saw two very dim lights pointing up at me from the bottom of the lake. This turned out to be the headlights of the vehicle. I called over my police radio for assistance, but I received no answer. It became clear that my police radio would not work out in the county. I had no idea how long it would take before my backup came, much less any ambulance that might be needed. *Now what*, I thought?

A feeling overcame me, one that I have felt before, talking to me in some strange way. Could this be my family trait talking to me? Could courage communicate with a chosen few? All I knew was that people were trapped in a car at the bottom of the lake, and I was the only policeman out there. I took off my gun belt, my bulletproof vest, my boots, and my police uniform top. All I had on was a black turtleneck shirt and my police issue pants. I waded out into the lake and tried my best to keep my eyes on the dim headlights, which I could barely see.

As I wadded further into the lake, I started getting into deeper water. Just then, I lost my footing and went head-deep into the lake. I then realized that the haze was back over the lake, and I had now lost eye contact with the two dim headlights. I still had some idea of where the car was submerged, but I could not be sure. I thought to myself, *I could use the headlights on the squad car to maybe help guide me to the car*, so I got out of the lake, soaking wet, and aimed the squad car headlights over the lake. Finally, I could hear police sirens coming down the road. I felt a little better, but I was still concerned for the people trapped in the submerged car. As I got back to the bank of the lake and prepared to go back in, my patrol sergeant, along with other officers, arrived. The patrol sergeant called to me, "Jack, what do you have?"

"There are a pair of dim headlights coming from the bottom of the lake!" I yelled back.

"Jack," he said, "it's too deep. Let's think of another way."

He was concerned about me. Since it was dark and the water was very deep, it would be very difficult to rescue anyone. My patrol sergeant could tell I was soaking wet, and he sent a couple of the other officers to the other end of the lake where the boat launch was. "Maybe we can use one of the boats over there to float out to where the submerged car is," he said.

This was a good idea, because in the end, the submerged car was over five hundred yards away, and at least twenty-feet down. That would make it a tough swim for me or anyone else who dared to venture out there, but we would only have been able to tell that when daylight finally broke.

At last, some officers returned with a little two-man boat. Still feeling that I was a part of this whole thing, I volunteered to go out in the boat. Another officer named John Rigdon said he would go too, so John and I got in the boat and paddled out until we were right above the car. Just then, our patrol sergeant said a scuba diver had arrived, and that we were to wait for him to go into the lake. I did not really blame the patrol sergeant because, after all, if John or myself got hurt in any way, he, as the supervisor, would have to account for our safety.

The scuba diver finally made his way out to where John and I were floating above the car. Bubbles suddenly appeared from the scuba diver as he came up from under the water right along side our boat. He took his mask off and said, "No one's in the car."

I said, "What do you mean, no one's in the car?"

"Just what I said. There's no one inside the car."

As it turned out, the car had been reported stolen. This must have been a way the suspect thought to get rid of car so that no one could trace it back to him. Man! I was so mad! John and I started paddling back to the lake's bank, and I noticed I felt a little different. I had lost track of time, and it turned out that I had unwittingly been involved in this whole incident that took over an hour and a half to resolve. I had been on the boat for about thirty minutes with wet clothes.

I felt extremely cold, and noticed that I was having some difficulty breathing. I heard a wheezing sound coming out of me. As soon as John and I arrived at the lake's shore, my patrol sergeant sent me over to where the rescue ambulance was standing by so I could be checked out.

When I walked over to the ambulance, one of the medics noticed I had a very pale look to my face. She asked, "How're you feeling?"

"Cold, very cold," I said.

The medic placed me in the ambulance and took my body temperature. She told me that my body temperature was two degrees away from hypothermia. She and the other medics transported me to the hospital, where I stayed for over two hours. They monitored me, and later explained that they had to get my body temperature back up to normal before I could leave the hospital. I never knew how cold a person could get until that night. I could not feel my fingers or my toes for several hours.

Nevertheless, putting my own safety at risk was something I had not even considered. I honestly thought there were people trapped in the submerged car. Instead, I had only discovered a stolen vehicle. I did not even get a thank you from the victim of the stolen car, and I almost ended up with hypothermia. I can only surmise that this test in life would follow me in my search for that inherited family trait of courage that I hoped would soon be identified through my career. Thus far, it has left me with only memories of what I thought a good cop should be. Here I am, a professional policeman—or law enforcement officer, whichever one you prefer—trying to make it home every night while at the same time searching for honor, bravery, and courage, to possibly bring some kind of balance in my life. Did my father instill this search in me? Was the desire to become this courageous person I hoped to someday be the result of brainwashing? It was obvious to me that law enforcement definitely suited me. Perhaps the seed was planted back in the recesses of my mind from when Father expressed a possible interest in law enforcement for himself from time-to-time.

Not long after the hypothermia incident, I was offered a position on the police department Gang Unit. The unit was called "SMASH." This stood for the acronym "serious matters acquire serious help." Only the very elite police officers were offered such a position. I felt very honored to be selected. This could have meant that someone in the department thought highly of me.

There was more good news when it turned out that my best friend on the force, Neal Haskins, was also offered a position on the unit. Neal and I had been hired at the police department at the same time, and we always hung out outside of work. We had drifted apart when I went to narcotics, and upon my return to patrol, we were assigned to different shifts. Now, we would finally be able to work together.

The SMASH Unit, basically your average S.W.A.T. team, dealt with street gangs and havoc, or extreme behavior not usually associated with average police patrol duties. We might get the "crazy call," named for a suicide jumper, a bomb threat, or even a need for some kind of "sting" operation. You might say the entire SMASH Unit could be crazier and less structured than the normal patrolman's beat.

Neal and I had to make sure we were always partners in the SMASH Unit. The head of the unit was Leon Cook, a police veteran with lots of knowledge on all the local gangs operating in the city. Leon knew how close friends Neal and I were, and he always tried to pair us up when we reported for our duty assignments every afternoon. All the other SMASH officers knew of the close friendship between Neal and I too, and they did not mind us partnering up.

The typical street detail in a day with the SMASH Unit would include all assigned SMASH Unit officers doing what we called a "street sweep," where we broke off in pairs and covered our area in the city, combing for gang members and drug dealers wanted on arrest warrants. All but two SMASH members would do this. Those two SMASH officers would be assigned to drive the patty wagon, basically a transport unit for that shift, that took all suspects arrested by the other SMASH officers to the local jailhouse.

No one in the SMASH Unit liked this detail, because for the entire shift, they exclusively picked up suspects already arrested, and they transported them to the jailhouse where they were then booked. Not a very exciting detail when you support an elite SMASH Unit.

The good news was that Neal and I would never have to do this detail, because we were so aggressive on the streets and made so many high profile arrests. Leon knew that putting us on the transport detail would only take us away from the more important job of getting bad guys off the streets.

One time, though, Neal and I had to do the transport detail after we had just gotten out on the streets. We had seen a drug deal go down, which led to an instant foot chase through the heavy populated city blocks. It was no big deal, until the suspect ran across the street and caused two cars to have an accident. Both of us continued the foot chase until we finally apprehended the bad guy. Everything seemed to be okay, until Leon told us he had to take us off the streets for that day.

"Why?" I asked.

"Both you guys do a good job," said Leon, "but one of those people in that car accident has turned out to be the mayor's wife, and the mayor probably won't understand what's just happened. He may think that if you and Neal had not chased that guy, then there wouldn't have been an accident."

"But, we're just doing our jobs. It was the bad guy, if anyone, who made the car accident happen."

"I know, and I agree," said Leon, "but my hands are tied. I just think it's better if you and Neal do the transport detail tonight and let things calm down for now."

Well, what could I say? I mean, he was the head of the SMASH Unit, and what he said went. So Neal and I had to drive the stupid patty wagon all over the city, taking the arrested suspects to the jailhouse and booking them in.

Fun, fun, fun. I am a cop, not a taxi driver, I thought. How can I even think of finding honor, bravery, and courage driving around a bunch of bad guys who, at the most, would spend one night in jail? This was not why I joined the SMASH Unit, let alone the police department. Neal thought the same way, and for the rest of the night, we tried to make jokes instead of dwelling on the undesirable detail we were elected to do.

The night passed by quickly because of Neal's wit, and he always made me laugh real easy. He had what I called a dry sense of humor, which struck me as extremely funny, because Neal had a very reserved personality. Neal was not as aggressive as me, and he was not a very big man, but whatever he lacked in height. weight, and aggression, he definitely made up in heart. Neal never backed down from anyone; however, it took him a lot longer to get physical, and he certainly had more patience than me.

Neal's compassion made him a really nice policeman who gave the bad guy every chance not to go to jail. I, on the other hand, would take a bad guy to jail for any reason and never give him another moment's thought. If they broke the law, then by golly, they went to jail. Neal and I had an interesting work relationship, because Neal always tried to get the bad guy to understand that what he did was wrong. I did not care if the bad guy realized it or not. Let the judge explain to him what he did wrong.

Watching Neal and I work demonstrated much drama as well as entertainment. Neal, the easy-going one, would always try and talk down a hostile situation. On the other hand, I encouraged the bad guy to "try us." If the bad guy thought he was tougher, I had to prove to him otherwise.

What was I thinking working in the SMASH Unit? What about my policeman career? I probably should have been more like Neal, except for the one and only time we had to transport the suspects to jail. Like I said, Neal had a great sense of humor, but sometimes he would go too far with his jokes and involve the suspects we were transporting.

On one occasion, Neal was driving, and he started swerving the transport van back and forth over the road, pretending he was dizzy and trying to make the prisoners feel uncomfortable. It worked, and as we finally pulled up to the back of the jailhouse, you could tell the prisoners were extremely unhappy with me, and especially Neal. As we escorted the prisoners inside the jailhouse, I noticed there were only two female jailers working that night. I also noticed there were several unsecured prisoners standing around in line waiting to be processed. This certainly did not represent the proper structure for a jailhouse.

The policy for the jailhouse was that all prisoners were to either be in handcuffs or shackles as they waited to be processed. The transporting officers always checked in their duty issued firearms at the secured lockers, so when the officer escorted a prisoner into the jailhouse, they were basically unarmed. This was why it was so important to have all prisoners secure.

As we walked into the jailhouse that night, none of the prisoners were secure. There must have been at least fifteen prisoners walking around unsecured, just like we were at a family picnic. This made me feel really uncomfortable, and I knew Neal felt the same way. The last thing you wanted would be to let any of the prisoners know you were scared or uneasy.

The streets have simple rules, and they are all based on respect. Any time a bad guy gets the upper hand on a policeman, he gets what he thinks, in his eyes, is respect from other street criminals.

We waited along with our prisoners, which we made sure were handcuffed. One of the already processed prisoners who had not been handcuffed made a comment. He looked at Neal and said, "What's wrong cop? Are you scared?" He referred to Neal and I, because we were the only policemen in the jailhouse in the vicinity of about fifteen unsecured prisoners, and they knew there were only two female jailers to process them.

"Why are the prisoners unsecured?" I asked the jailers. "We've run out of handcuffs."

An un-handcuffed prisoner made a comment to me. He said, "Can't you take care of yourself without that big gun y'all carry?"

Before I could reply to his smart-ass remark, Neal said, "The only thing we are scared of is running out of all you bad guys to arrest."

That did it. The next thing I knew, I got hit in the side of the face, and the whole jailhouse became very unstable. Now, the guy who hit me got in a cheap shot. He blind-sided me, and I thought to myself, *That was a very cowardly thing to do.* I knew then he did not have the heart to take me, so the ole Mayfield blood got to boiling, and I fought back. The end result was that the cowardly prisoner spent the night in the jailhouse infirmary, and I had to go to the emergency room and receive nine stitches in the right ear, where he had gotten in his one and only cheap shot.

After it was all over with, Neal and I realized we were very lucky. That bad guy turned out to be the first and the last one to ever try and attack us. Surely, if the other unsecured prisoners would have joined in, Neal and I might not be here today. We have the man above to thank for that.

That night Neal said, "I'm glad we were together when the fight broke out."

In sarcastic tone, I said, "Appreciate that. I mean, it's not like we instigated it."

Neal laughed, and I joined in. After all, we were not just partners; we were also best friends.

Chapter Nine

Chasing Courage

To continue my undeniable search for courage, I became aware that I must endure the ever-present events in my life. I thought the SMASH Unit was just right for me, but after a short tour of duty and now the scar on my right ear, I realized that settling down to a specific assigned position would bring me fulfillment and balance in my life. The position I had in mind brought me back to the good old patrol. I really never had too many disappointing events in patrol, well, except the ceiling incident and the out of control car. Oh yeah, do not forget the hypothermia thing. Nevertheless, I wanted to do patrol. Going back to patrol would be very quiet. It would be easier to stay out of the trouble that could land me in the hospital emergency room, or even worse, the Chief's office.

Let us face it, as a policeman, whether a rookie cop or an old-timer, you were going to get into trouble. You might not end up in the emergency room at the hospital, but more likely than not, as a policeman, you would eventually be sent to the Chief's office. Furthermore, the old-timers used to tell me that when you got sent to the Chief's office or complained about anything in any way, that simply meant you were working and doing your job. As the saying goes, "You can't please all the people all of the time." This breaks down to that idea that if you were a good cop, and doing a good job, some people in general would be upset with you. It might be the speeder who did not know that driving fast was dangerous, or maybe a drunk guy in front of the grocery store who did not know he was bad for business, or even the jaywalker who thought there was nothing wrong with a shortcut.

All in all, complaints would definitely out-weigh praise. Oh, the rewards of being a policeman!

My utmost intentions were to get back to patrol and back to the midnight shift. Unexpectedly, I received notice to return to patrol, but I would be going to the evening shift, working the hours of 3:00 p.m. until 11:00 p.m. This shift was called the rock 'n' roll shift, and only the young, gung-ho policemen worked this shift, because most of the crazy stuff usually happened during the hours of 3:00 p.m. and 11:00 p.m.

Blasted, now I have done it! I would be stuck on a shift with policemen who liked to mix it up and get into every exciting and dangerous thing they could. This was kind of how I used to be before I realized police work was not a game, and I was tired of getting hurt and getting into trouble. I received the reputation of being a "crazy cop" when I did aggressive police work. I had become more mature and laid back, and I hoped my patrolman peers would be able to see that. I want to be passive and just try and do my job without the old cowboy cop in me coming out.

As I came to terms with my assignment, I reported to work for roll call. My new supervisor was Sergeant Morris, a twenty-three-year veteran with the department. After my first roll call on the rock 'n' roll shift, Sergeant Morris called me in his office and said, "Jack, I want a smooth sailing shift."

"I understand," I explained. "I intend on being out of sight, out of mind, and out of trouble."

My reputation was going to be hard to live down, but in order for me to stay on patrol, I was told I should not try to act like a so-called "cowboy" or "crazy cop."

"Jack," said Sergeant Morris, "I want everything 'by the book.'"

The problem would be if some of the other officers would think less of me if I did not live up to my youthful reputation.

For weeks and weeks, I reported to the rock 'n' roll shift, and eventually, I began to hear talk in the police station's hallways. I would hear snickers and rude comments like: "Officer Mayfield is not as brave as I thought he was;" "Officer Mayfield acts as if he is scared to patrol and answer calls;" "Officer Mayfield acts like he is a timid rabbit instead of a fighting tiger."

These comments began to take a toll on me. I went from having the respect and admiration of my fellow officers and peers, to having them believe I was a washed-up policeman who was scared to do my job. The other officers actually thought I dodged calls from dispatch and avoided dangerous situations. I have to be honest; they were, in fact, right.

It had nothing to do with being scared. I just did not want to take a chance on getting hurt anymore, and I did not want to take a chance on getting into any more trouble. The sergeant had already warned me to be laid-back, and I did just that.

I had planned to continue my reserved demeanor until one day, when I reported to work and roll call to get my car unit and territory for that day, and the Sergeant passed out a "hot sheet."

A "hot sheet" was a list of every vehicle stolen from the local area and surrounding cities. It gave a description of the stolen vehicle and also a possible tag number for each. When a police officer located a stolen car, more likely than not, a hot-pursuit car chase ensues. This is a very dangerous situation, because most people that flee from the police by vehicle are very crazy, and have no concern for the safety of others.

The officer that chases a running car runs the risk of getting into an accident and getting seriously hurt—a big risk I was not willing to take. I took my copy of the "hot sheet" and put it in the glove box of my squad car. I decided not to be anywhere around or near a car chase. Finding a stolen vehicle would be the last thing on my mind. After all, it would bring me unwanted attention.

One day, a story circulated from the morning shift about a stolen white Chevy Camaro that police had chased earlier. The driver of the white Camaro out-ran and out-drove the police officers. He was crazy, of course, because he did not have the policies and guidelines to adhere to in a car pursuit like the officers did. See, we have to abide by the traffic laws as well as the criminal laws. This puts many constraints on us, but the crazy driver does not care about that; he only wants to escape from the police.

At roll call, Sergeant Morris said, "The driver of the white Camaro car-jacked a female and took her car. He is also wanted for armed robbery in another city nearby. The white Camaro was seen this morning in the southwest part of town, and I'm sure he's still around somewhere."

Before I was able to drive away from the police station, Sergeant Morris called for me to report to his office. When I approached his door, he said, "Officer Mayfield, this is a police cadet that's going to observe police duties with you tonight."

A police cadet! This was like being a boy scout, only with the police department. After a police cadet passes certain tests, they are allowed to ride in a squad car with a patrolman chosen by the supervisor. The police cadet could not get out of the vehicle on calls; however, he could monitor the police radio and see what went on in the city from a police officer's perspective.

I looked at the police cadet and said, "Hello, call me Jack."

"My name is Henry, and I always wanted to be a policeman," said the police cadet.

"How old are you?" I asked.

"Sixteen," Henry said.

There was no concern on my part about having a sixteen-year-old police cadet riding around with me because, after all, there would be no more of the "cowboy" cop I used to be. I patrolled and made sure the public saw me. That was all. "Henry," I said, "this is probably going to be a real boring night for you."

"No," said Henry, "it's not, Officer Mayfield. I have heard all about you."   "What did you hear about me?" I asked.

"I heard in our cadet meetings that you're one of the best cops on the force, and that you're not afraid of anything," said Henry.

"Believe me, Henry, those are just stupid rumors that are not true," I said, though he did not buy it one bit.

As Henry and I got into the squad car, he asked with a huge smile on his face, "Where to first?"

"I have an every-day routine," I explained, "that I plan on sticking to, and that means going and getting a big cup of coffee in the very northeast part of the city." I continued to explain, "The northeast part of the city is the safest and quietist part of the whole town. There is hardly ever anything bad happening up there."

As I finished explaining our tour of duty and my intentions, Henry said, "That's fine, we have all night to get into something."

Henry obviously did not take my explanation of the night's events very seriously. My game plan involved *not* getting into any trouble, but so as not to make him feel bad, I said, "Sure, kid. Whatever you say."

As Henry and I drove down the street heading for the Stop n' Shop to get my cup of coffee, a voice came over the police radio. "Attention, all units! Attention, all units! The stolen white Camaro has been seen in the southern part of the city around the Stop n' Shop convenience store."

The next thing I knew, all the officers on duty acknowledged to the dispatcher that they were en route to that location, all except one police officer.

Unfortunately, I pretended not to hear anything over the police radio. To my dismay, good ole Henry was there to let me know what the dispatcher said. He said, "Officer Mayfield, aren't we going to respond to that call about the stolen white Camaro?"

"No," I said. "There are enough police officers already going that way."

"But, what if they need some help?" Henry said.

I could see the disappointment clear as day on Henry's face. Somehow, I had to break it to him; I was not the same cop he heard about.

At that moment, I wondered what had happened to me. Had I lost my nerve? Could I be scared like the other police officers believed? What happened to the Mayfield blood in me? Where was the honor, bravery, and the missing courage I longed for? It now became a nightmare to me.

At one time, I decided with determination to find my inherited family trait, which I truly believed was courage. But now, staying safe and staying as far away from danger and confrontations became important. I did not even consider myself to be a man, much less a true Mayfield man. Maybe courage eluded me after all, and maybe being afraid of appearing as a plain, normal guy had become my greatest fear. How could I know for sure? What would it take to show me?

Before the call came through over the police radio, it was obvious from Henry's face that he admired the image of what a good policeman should be. Now, after the call, it could be possible that Henry may not want to ever be a cop anymore when he grew up. I had inflicted a slacker's mentality on myself, and now I may have adversely influenced a sixteen-year-old police cadet. Something had to give. There had to be some kind of old school police blood still in this Mayfield heart.

I got to the middle of a nearby intersection, spun the squad car around, and said, "Okay, Henry, we will head to the area where the stolen white Camaro is, just in case any of the other police officers need our help, but we won't get in a car chase, so don't get your hopes up about that."

Boy! Henry became very excited, as if he had just had a birthday and got the biggest and best present ever. His face lit up like a Christmas tree.

As we headed southwest, I listened closely to the police radio and monitored what was occurring. While we sped toward the chase with our car lights and siren on, one of the other police officers broke into the police radio saying that he had located the stolen white Camaro and was now involved in a high-speed chase. The police officer indicated his twenty as he rapidly chased the recklessly driven Camaro up and down various streets. He also said, "The driver is a white male with dirty blonde hair." In just about all cases, the chased car runs stop signs and traffic lights, and the patrolman must follow the best he can. Other policemen try to reach the areas being broadcast over the police radio. In these chases, the criminal often side-swipes other cars or runs them off the road.

The police radio went completely silent. The pursuing officer broke in again and said, "I lost him. He got away."

The Sergeant spoke over the police radio and asked, "What's the last known direction the white Camaro was going?"

"Northeast," said the patrolman.

I thought for a moment. If the stolen white Camaro headed northeast and Henry and I were heading southwest, I guessed what would happen next. Sure enough, the stolen white Camaro passed right by my squad car, going in the other direction.

It happened again; that feeling in my stomach, the one I had experienced so many times; that being a Mayfield feeling. I had to be a better man than the bad guy driving the stolen white Camaro. I immediately spun the car around in the middle of the street, and then I radioed dispatch to identify myself and to give my twenty. "I am right behind it," I said.

Sergeant Morris' voice came over the police radio saying, "Officer Mayfield, do *not* pursue the car. You have a police cadet with you, and you're not authorized to engage the stolen vehicle."

I could not stop myself. Any other day, I might have heeded what Sergeant Morris said, but on this day, the "crazy cowboy" cop came out, and I chased the stolen white Camaro all over the city for at least fifteen city blocks. Henry sat upright in the passenger seat enjoying the hell out of this most awesome police car chase. In and out of traffic we went, over road medians and on top of street sidewalks the wrong way down one-way streets. I must say, it was challenging just to keep up with this Camaro. This guy was determined. He might have out-driven all the other police officers earlier, but no way would he get away from me.

It could have been that Mayfield blood just popping its head back up in my life. I felt rejuvenated at this point, like a new man. An unbelievable adrenaline rush coursed through my veins.

All I could think of was how this guy car-jacked some defenseless woman, and then went on to hold-up a liquor store. Evidently, he thought of himself as "bad news;" another "would be" tough guy. Whatever the appropriate adjective to describe him was, dangerous definitely fit best. If I did not get him, he would most likely hurt somebody else.

No way could I let that happen.

Little did I know what would come next. As I continued to pursue the stolen white Camaro, we ended up on a state highway that ran right through the city. No more than a car-length away and reaching at least ninety miles an hour, we closed the gap on the stolen car. We noticed a sheriff's deputy standing on the road beside his patrol car that he had pulled off to the side of the road.

I thought, *What in the world is he doing?* He probably heard about the car chase that was in progress over a police scanner, and he might have thought he could help in some way. *Why is he out of his patrol car?* I wondered. The officer stood only about one hundred yards in front of us, but we were closing the gap fast. Then, I saw the deputy do something. He slung something across the road as the stolen white Camaro and our police car raced toward him. *What was that*, I thought?

Then, it hit me. It was police "stop sticks." Stop sticks were spikes used to flatten tires of cars fleeing from the police during car chases. Because we were too close to the white Camaro, it was obvious that the stop sticks were going to catch both the Camaro and our car. There was not enough time for the deputy to broadcast what he was doing so as not to cause me any danger. It was just too late. In a split second, just as the deputy threw out the stop sticks, the stolen white Camaro ran over the spikes and immediately went out of control. Seconds later, our car followed suit. I fought like crazy to keep the squad car under control. I held onto the steering wheel with both hands so as not to lose it. I thought, *This can't be happening. We're the good guys; we aren't supposed to get hurt.*

As I saw the stolen white Camaro spin out of control and come to rest in the middle of the street, I realized that *my* squad car was out of control. Henry and I spun in the direction of a huge bridge. Henry held on for dear life. If we did not hit the bridge, we would probably end up crashing off the top of the embankment into a shallow creek below the bridge. I had to think quickly. *The bridge or the creek? Which one?*

No matter what decision I made, we were going to get hurt; I just did not know how badly. At the last moment, as the bridge was nearing, I yanked the steering wheel one more time to the right as hard as I could and took the chance of crashing into the creek. I figured the creek may be better than hitting the concrete bridge. The squad car went airborne, landing nose-first into the shallow creek below.

Just as we landed in the creek, it felt as though the front of the car was going to flip forward and the top of the car would become the bottom of the car, possibly sending Henry and me into a tragic conclusion. Instead, the back tires slammed back to the ground from the momentum of the impact. The car sat upright in the normal position. Thank God, Henry and I were all right. To this day, I tell everyone that God must have sent an angel to push the back of the car down so we would not flip forward. If the car had flipped forward, Henry and I might have drowned or worse. We might not be here today. The Lord certainly watched over us that day.

When the vehicle finally came to its resting place, I noticed that my police badge was lying on the dashboard of the car. Henry had squatted down as close as he could get to the floorboard. The next thing I remembered was the ambulance medics taking Henry's and my blood pressure, which they took several times before finally transporting us to the local hospital for observation. The whole accident happened so fast, I had forgotten about the bad guy possibly getting away. Shock sets in after an accident like we had, and one tends to be dazed and out of touch with their surroundings.

At the hospital, my shift officers came to check on Henry and me. That was when I found out that the bad guy had, in fact, been captured. He not only had a firearm in the car with him, but he also had the stolen money from the armed robbery he had committed earlier. What a relief! The bad guy had not out-done me. I am a Mayfield man, supposedly above and beyond that of a normal man. If I had in any way allowed the bad guy to out-do me, mounds of shame would have overwhelmed me. If the bad guy *had* gotten away, it would *not* have been my fault in this particular situation. I never wanted any of the bad guys to get away; that attitude is what drove me to be an excellent cop.

In this situation, everything was under control until the irresponsible deputy threw the spikes across the road. He could see how close we were. He should have radioed to another officer up ahead about the situation and said that perhaps the stop sticks might not have been a good idea at that point in time, especially as close as the Camaro and I were in proximity. Sure, it caused the bad guy to wreck, but it also caused Henry and I to go nose-first into the creek. We could have died.

Besides my squad car being totaled, a yield sign that I drove over before going off the road ended up piercing the hood of the car and was stuck there.

When I came back to reality, I remembered that Sergeant Morris had ordered me to break off the car chase. He also reminded me that I had a police cadet riding with me, and his safety was foremost a priority.

While in the hospital, Sergeant Morris came to check on us. He said to me, "Officer Mayfield, as soon as you're released from the hospital, you need to come directly to my office." Those words cut through me like a knife. Just as I started to act like a good cop again, started doing my job to catch the bad guys, it now looked as if I had done the opposite.

As Sergeant Morris left the hospital, Henry's mother came to see him. She heard what had happened and became frantic about her son. How could anyone blame her? This was her sixteen-year-old kid supposedly in the hands of responsible policemen. The families of policemen have this concern, too; that their loved one may not make it home safely.

When she found out Henry was okay, she came in my room and said, "Officer Mayfield, thank you for keeping Henry safe."

"I'm so sorry about the wreck," I explained to her.

She simply said, "If he wasn't with you, he might well have been seriously hurt. All that my son has ever wanted was to be a policeman, and if you had dropped him off or had not done your job, Henry might be less of a policeman.

We have taught Henry that to be a policeman means being a good person who takes care of others."

I must say, this was one of the nicest compliments I ever received. I thought she would be mad because her son was hurt in a high-speed police car chase; however, she acted as though she was so proud of Henry. For the first time in many years, I realized that some people actually do like policemen, even when they do not need them.

The good news is that Henry and I were released from the hospital, both of us only sustaining minor cuts and bruises; no doubt, a true blessing. After Henry left with his mother, an officer waited to give me a ride back to the police station and to what I thought would be my punishment from Sergeant Morris.

Upon arriving at the station, I gathered up some nerve, knowing he had to face Sergeant Morris. This moment reminded me of when I was that little boy who had to face Mr. G.L. Thatcher for that broken glass door. The difference this time involved an entire police squad car. I hoped that I would have the courage to face the very worst in this case.

I walked to Sergeant Morris' office and stood at the door. My sergeant looked up and said, "Come in and shut the door, Jack." I took a seat and braced myself as Sergeant Morris continued. "Do you know you disobeyed a direct order? Do you know you could've killed that police cadet, or yourself?" This did not look good. I continued to brace myself for the toughest ass-chewing ever. "You're through in law enforcement, Jack. I will make sure you never get a promotion or a good assignment ever again, if I can help it." Shock came over me as Sergeant Morris finished the ass-chewing. "And, Officer Mayfield, if you don't know it by now, there are no more cowboys in the world."

Getting the bad guy off the streets certainly classifies as an awesome feat, since he out-ran all the other police, I thought.

The bad guy certainly met his match in me, and catching him probably prevented other serious crimes from happening in the future. The voice in my head resounded the phrase, "No just cause goes unpunished." To me, that summed it all up. *At least I didn't get fired*, I thought. *I'll probably be on foot patrol for the remainder of my career.* One thing was for sure; all the other patrolmen started looking at me differently, like they had when I first started. That was a kind of admiration that only other policemen have for one another. This helped heal my wounds and the depression that set in after Sergeant Morris made me feel like the criminal, and the bad guy look like the victim.

To me, the aftermath looked like the direct result of me being a Mayfield. My true self kept bursting though. Sometimes, one had to go against policy and procedures. I expected something different from my disobedience of Sergeant Morris' orders. I tried to find my balance in life, my heritage, my courage; things that I have yet to capture. To be brave also means to be lucky. There was a saying I often heard, "Luck is an ally to the brave," but I had to feel and know inside, beyond a shadow of a doubt, that I possessed the same honor, bravery, and courage that my father and grandfather had. I could only wonder if my luck would hold.

Chapter Ten

Sixth Sense

After the last episode in my law enforcement duties, I had to take a long look at what my true goals and dreams were. I wanted to be rich, that was a given. I wanted to be famous, not infamous. I wanted to have a balance in my life, and to discover that I was a true Mayfield man with honor, bravery, and, most importantly, the family trait of courage. This became the ultimate goal for my life. I knew I'd never become rich as a policeman, nor would I ever expect to be famous. I did believe that a balance in my life would directly correlate with the important family trait. I believed the search would take place in this profession; that the inherited family characteristic would develop though my work in law enforcement.

Through my police profession, I discovered one trait uncommon to most. It was a sixth sense, a person's intuition, or as we policemen call it, a "gut feeling." That sixth sense or gut feeling often directed me to react or not to react. Maybe it's a gift from above. Maybe it's a warning sign to some degree. Whatever the case, my sixth sense helped me out in a lot of different ways.

The most dramatic way happened when I was being trained as a new policeman. I was doing our normal routine patrol with my training officer, John, when Captain Emerson requested we meet him in the parking lot of a gas station off Fifth Street. We did what we were told and pulled into the parking lot of the gas station, and then we waited on Captain Emerson. He was the captain in charge of all arrest warrants. He was not our official supervisor, although he was still a captain. His duty included making sure that all active arrest warrants were served and processed. As John and I waited, Captain Emerson finally arrived. He spoke exclusively to my training officer, as I was only a rookie.

"John, I have an arrest warrant for this guy named Jeff Parks. He abused his wife two days ago and fractured her jaw. She's very afraid of him, and she had her jaw wired together after the injury. She did come in and sign warrants on him for domestic violence, and she will testify in court. However, she doesn't want him to know until then that she signed the charges."

The Captain reiterated what the woman said. "He'll be home tonight between 5:00 p.m. and 6:00 p.m. for dinner. After he eats, he usually leaves and goes off drinking somewhere."

The Captain continued, "I want you two guys to go along with Officer Jake and his partner to 704 43rd Avenue, and arrest this bad guy so that she can at least feel safe tonight."

John told Captain Emerson, "No problem."

We left the gas station, and John used the police radio to contact Officer Jake and his new rookie partner, Tim. John asked them to meet us about 5:15 p.m. at the address of 704

43rd Avenue. We had about twenty minutes before we were supposed to meet Jake and Tim as we drove around.

"Jack," said John, "have you ever arrested anyone for domestic violence, yet?"

"No, why do you ask?" I said.

"Guys who hit ladies, or any women, for that matter, are all cowards," he said. "They are still dangerous because they think it's their woman, and they can do whatever they want to them. You be careful, Jack, and be aware that this guy, Jeff Parks, must like getting physical since he hits his wife."

"I'm ready for anything," I said. "We really need to get this guy and put him behind bars, tonight."

John and I discussed the domestic violence arrest we were fixing to make, and then John noticed it was time to head to the address and meet with Officer Jake and his partner, Tim. We got to the address, parked the squad car a block down the road, and turned off the car lights. We saw Officer Jake and his partner pull in right behind us. All of us exited our vehicles, and John gave Officer Jake and Tim a briefing on what we were going to do.

"The guy's name is Jeff Parks," said John. "He's wanted for domestic violence against his wife. He hit her in the jaw and fractured it, and her jaw had to be wired shut. He's supposed to be eating inside, right about now, and Mrs. Parks is expecting us, but Jeff Parks doesn't have any idea we're coming. Mrs. Parks is very afraid of him, so don't let him know that she's the one who signed the charges on him for domestic violence."

Officer Jake and Tim acknowledged they understood the game plan, and John also told them to be careful of the guy.

"He might try to resist and get away when we find him, so take precautions and do this by the book," said John.

After this, Officer Jake and Tim went to the back of the house. John and I went to the front. John rang the doorbell, and Mrs. Parks opened the door. John said, "Hello. We're here looking for Jeff Parks."

"He's not here; he just left," said Mrs. Parks.

I thought, *How could this be?*

She knew we were coming, and she knew we were going to arrest him. Suspiciously, I thought he might be inside hiding, so I asked Mrs. Parks, "Do you mind if we search your house?"

Without any hesitation, Mrs. Parks said, "Why sure, officer, come on in and search the whole house."

John and I went inside, and John called Officer Jake and Tim to come in and help search the very big house. It could have been about 2,400 square feet. There were five bedrooms and three baths. John and I waited for Jake and Tim to come into the living room. All united now, we split up, with John telling everyone, "Be careful."

I went straight to a bedroom just off the hallway of the living room. As I entered the bedroom, I noticed the bed in the middle of the room and the bed's skirting that hung really low on the floor. My first thought was to look under the bed. This seemed like the most common place in which someone would hide. I got on my knees, bent over, and raised the bed skirting just enough to look under it. Suddenly, my sixth sense took hold. Something told me the guy was definitely hiding in that bedroom, but in some other place. There was a closet with a cloth curtain as a door on the other side of the bed. I just knew Jeff Parks was hiding in that closet.

I got up and went over to the closet, and with one quick motion, I pulled the cloth curtain open to see only clothes. What just happened? I knew he was going to be in there. My sixth sense told me he was there. My sixth sense had never been wrong before. I searched the entire closet to find nothing but clothes. I felt so helpless.

Just then, John called for me and said, "John, he's not here. I guess we'll come back another day."

Mrs. Parks escorted us to the front door. We all walked back to our parked squad cars at the end of the block. I still sensed Parks was hiding in that house. Maybe Mrs. Parks hid him out of fear. My gut feeling still talked to me.

As we walked back to our cars, I said, "I just know Parks is hiding inside that house."

"I agree," said John, "but we'll have to get him another time."

"Why wait 'till later?" I asked. "That poor lady's probably so scared right now, and I know he's in there."

Officer Jake and Tim had a "whatever" look on their faces.

"We're leaving," said Officer Jake. "You do what you want."

Officer Jake and Tim got into their squad car and drove off. John looked at me with a huge smile on his face and said, "Well, Jack, what do you want to do?"

"Let's go get him," I said.

"Okay, then, let's go get him," said John.

We walked back to the house, my sixth sense working overtime. I had a very unusual, sick feeling in my stomach. Nevertheless, the gut feeling told me to be careful, and that the bad guy was definitely in that house. As John and I walked onto the porch, I knocked twice on the front door.

"Who is it?" asked Mrs. Parks.

"It's the police again," I said.

She came to the door and asked, "Is something wrong?"

"There's one more place I would like to check," I said, "if you don't mind."

Hesitantly she said, "Oh, okay, just give me a minute."

I knew for sure now that Parks was in the house. We totally surprised him this time. He might have known we were coming the first time, but not now. I could hear fear in Mrs. Parks' voice, but also relief. The Mayfield blood stirred inside me again, the one that told me I was better than this woman-beater. I fed off the unknown, unfamiliar urge to prove that I was a better man—a Mayfield man.

Mrs. Parks finally opened the door, and I went immediately to the bedroom where I had gotten the initial feeling that Parks was hiding. As I entered the bedroom, I looked at the bed with the low-hanging bed skirt, and then I looked directly at the closet with the cloth curtain door. In one quick motion, I leaped over the bed, grabbed the cloth curtain with one hand, and pulled it straight back. That's when I found him. He had a look of fear on his face. He knew why I was there, and he knew it was time to pay the piper. I grabbed the spineless wife beater, spun him around, and handcuffed him faster than a cowboy ropes a calf. I must have been talking loudly, because John heard all the commotion and rushed to help me. Both of us escorted Jeff Parks through the house, and as we passed by Mrs. Parks, we stopped in front of her.

"If you *ever* lay another hand on her, Jeff, I will lay my hands on you," I said as we walked Jeff out to the squad car and escorted him directly to jail.

When John and I got back to the station, Officer Jake and his partner, Tim, hung their heads low.

"We're all on the same team, and we'll all get credit for this arrest," I told them.

"But," said Officer Jake, "we left you and John."

"You didn't leave us," I said. "You were just being available to help someone else." Then I walked away.

Later, John came up and said, "How did you know?"

"How did I know what?" I said.

"How did you know he was hiding in the closet?" asked John.

"I just felt it," I said.

I never heard anything more about Mrs. Parks. I often wondered if Jeff Parks ever hit her again. At least for one night, I stopped him from abusing Mrs. Parks, and perhaps gave her some peace of mind, if just for a moment. How did I know he was hiding in that closet? There was no fear or worry of getting hurt. Could my search for the family trait be over? Could I have found the Mayfield courage at last? Still, if that were the case, would I not feel differently inside? Would I not know for sure that I was deserving of the Mayfield family name? Where were the answers?

These questions still remained in my life. I had not yet found the answers, and I have yet to find what I consider to be true bravery, honor, and the most important quality, courage.

Chapter Eleven

Promotion Time

After all my trials and tribulations in life, one would think I might have learned a few secret things that could help in guiding me with everyday routines. Unfortunately, I am still at that point in my life that every step I take is a learning one. This held true when, after years of service with the police department, I finally qualified for a promotional test. The test was for detective. This sounded so cool. I would get to wear clothes, a gold badge, and I would not have to chase bad guys on foot or in a vehicle anymore. It sounded like just the ticket. You see, police detectives respond to crimes after they occur. Most patrolmen are initial responders, and that sometimes means they have to get their hands dirty.

I thought, *At this point, I've already had my hands dirty enough. Why shouldn't I try and take advantage of this opportunity?* I did not think long before deciding to give it a shot.

I arrived early at the police station and prepared myself for the exam with at least forty-five other patrolmen and special duty officers hoping to get the title of Police Detective. The test was long and mentally draining.

I thought to myself, *Why does a police detective have to know all these questions on this test?* I mean, after all, you were a cop first and foremost. What difference did it make if you were a good test-taking cop? Then I thought, *The difference would be that a police detective should be able to solve puzzling crimes, and deal with situations requiring the ability to think and use different methods that might be unknown to an everyday patrolman.* After completing the test, I wondered how it went.

It was not enough that I still searched for my family traits of bravery, honor, and courage, but as a Mayfield, I was supposed to have some sense. Failing the exam would devastate me. I went home that day and dwelled on all the questions I answered first. I second-guessed myself, and I started thinking that if it was meant to be, it would come to pass. Hours later, I received a phone call. It was from the deputy chief of the entire police department, Deputy Chief Phillips.

"Officer Mayfield, this is Deputy Chief Phillips. I'm calling to tell you about the very high score you made on the written exam of the police detective test. If you're interested, we would like you to come in tomorrow afternoon for an interview."

Well, that did it! I yelled with excitement and danced around the room like it was Christmas Day. I had just gotten the present I had been longing for. I became really anxious. I reminded myself that I hadn't gotten the promotion yet, and heck, in my experience, if anything could go wrong, it usually did.

It was so hard to sleep that night anticipating the next day's interview for the promotion to police detective. The last thing I remembered before finally drifting off to sleep was the honor and prestige that came with wearing a gold badge.

Detective Mayfield, I thought to myself. *That has a nice ring to it.*

I went to sleep with visions of grandeur floating endlessly in my mind. If I did get this promotion, did it mean, out of the Mayfield family traits I searched for, that maybe I could finally scratch honor off my list? After all, a police officer had to be honorable in this day and age.

Even if I did find honor, what about bravery and that ever-powerful courage? This still drove constant turmoil in my life. No balance, no fulfillment inside, just the search. I awoke the next day like normal, but inside I felt so strange. I got dressed and proceeded down to the police station. It felt weird going to the police station when I did not have to. You know, like having to work, or bail somebody out, or with some people, finding a new cell mate. I just wanted to get the interview over with.

After arriving at the police station, I went directly to the office of Deputy Chief Phillips' and waited until he called for me. A stern but intriguing voice rang out from the inner office, "Officer Mayfield"

"Yes," I replied.

"Come in my office," Deputy Chief Phillips said.

As I entered the office, I first saw deputy Chief Phillips, then Councilman John Evans, and last but not least, Mayor Edward Hughes. "Take a seat, Officer Mayfield," Chief Phillips said. "The reason we're here today is to determine if you have the stuff to be a police detective."

Mayor Hughes started, "You see, Officer Mayfield, we know all about your history. First, falling through the ceiling of the police department, then practically getting hypothermia from a submerged vehicle with nobody in it, and last but not least, you cost the city money by totaling a perfectly good squad car during a police chase you were directly ordered not to be involved in. Why should you get the promotion to detective when your reputation is as a loose cannon; a cowboy that hasn't realized there is no place in law enforcement for rebels?"

I lowered my head, wondering how I would get the promotion after the mayor's recount of my activity as a policeman. Chief Phillips broke my thoughts and said, "Officer Mayfield, you are extremely intelligent, but quick to jump head first into most things. If you think you can use your mind over being a cowboy, we'll promote you, and it will be official starting tomorrow."

What a surprise! Stuttering a bit, I said, "Yes, sir. I would like very much to show I can use my mind and commit myself to proper law enforcement."

As I saw the Chief grin, I also heard the mayor say under his breath, "We'll see." The mayor has never had any confidence in me anyway, and to be honest, I did not care to impress him or the councilman, or even the chief for that matter.

All these years I tried to prove myself, to prove my worthiness of the Mayfield name. I have tried to find honor, bravery, and courage, and bring balance and peace into my life. Still, I felt empty inside. Obtaining the promotion to police detective would simply complicate things even more. As a police detective, I would not be able to show my bravery or courageousness. Detectives show up after the crime happens. My quest for inner courage and strength may never reveal itself.

What have I done? Taking the promotion might well have sealed my fate. Maybe I was just normal. Maybe I was just a plain southern man, working in no particular thing that would make me any different than, say, a person working in the produce section at your local grocery store.

Maybe I was not a true Mayfield. These thoughts made me feel so uncertain about a lot of things in my life. It was too late now. I had said yes and made a declaration. I would start tomorrow, and that was that.

So guess what? I would have a new training partner. When a policeman gets promoted to detective, they ride with veteran detectives. There you go, rookie world again. It sucked. Having several years as a cop under my belt would not lessen being treated like a babe in the woods. Oh well, just another part of my life. I would just have to suck it up.

My first day as a police detective was quite different than I expected. I first reported to the Investigation Division of the police department. The division had always been in the same station I worked in; however, only detectives were allowed in the Investigation Division area. Entering the secure location, I saw who was assigned to train me—Detective Earl Lewis. He looked like he was in his sixties. He wore a button-down shirt with an untied tie, and after I came in, he said to me, "You must be Officer—excuse me, Detective Mayfield."

"Yes, sir," I said.

"Son, don't call me sir; call me Earl," Detective Lewis said.

"Okay, Earl," I said. "You can call me Jack." Earl showed me around the office and walked me to my desk. I finally had my own desk! This started out great.

"Jack, you ready to go?" Earl said.

"Go where?" I said.

"We had a robbery last night," said Earl, "and we need to go talk with one of the witnesses."

"A robbery?" I asked dismayed.

"Yeah, a robbery," said Earl. "This makes the fifth one this week. It looks like it's going to be the same guy."

"How can you tell?" I asked.

"He does the same thing," said Earl. "He robs only liquor stores, and he uses a semi-automatic gun that he threatens the clerk with. He also makes the clerk lie down on the ground while he takes the money from the cash register."

"Do you have any suspects?" I asked.

"No," said Earl, "the only thing that we know is that he robs these stores about 4:00 in the afternoon, and he usually runs away on foot."

I thought, *Knowing my luck, we will more than likely ride right up on him while he is busy robbing some liquor store.* Little did I know that I was almost right.

As Earl and I drove to meet the witness in this prior robbery, the police dispatcher sent out a call over the police radio reporting a robbery that had just occurred. "Attention, all units! Attention, all units! A robbery just occurred at the package store on Forty-fifth Avenue. The only description given was a black male with a handgun."

Because we were detectives, we were usually requested *after* a robbery took place, and in this case, we were not even first responders. I had to learn this, because when the call came out, my normal instincts emerged, and I said to Earl, "Let's go! Let's go!"

"Don't get in a hurry," Earl said calmly. "You're a detective now, and you have to think and not just rush into everything."

"What do you mean?" I said.

"Listen to the radio. They didn't give a real good description for one, and you don't really know who you are looking for," responded Earl. "Any black male running down the road for any reason could be a suspect if you go by how the dispatchers described the suspect. Take your time and think."

"What we'll do now is head to the liquor store that was just robbed, see if the clerk can give a better description of the guy who just robbed them, and see if there's anything that needs to be processed."

"Processed" means taking pictures of a crime scene, fingerprints, or any evidence that might be helpful in solving the crime.

Earl and I arrived at the liquor store on Forty-fifth Avenue.

"Jack, get the fingerprint kit from the trunk of the car," Earl instructed. After I got the kit and walked back to where Earl was, we walked inside to check on the clerk. The clerk, a little old lady, was apparently scared half to death. She was crying and trying to remain calm. Earl asked, "Ma'am, do you need an ambulance?"

"No, I just want to go home," she said.

"Okay, but can you first tell me what happened?" said Earl.

"This guy walked in the store and pointed a gun at me. Then he told me to lie down on the ground and not to look at what he was doing," she said. "I could hear the cash register open, and then he said, 'If you move, I will kill you.' This was so terrifying, I just stayed there for at least five minutes after he left."

Earl stopped her there, and said, "Okay, okay. Do you know how much money he got?"

I thought to myself, *What was so important about that?*

"I think only about $100," the clerk said.

Earl thanked the clerk and said, "Come on, Jack. We got things to do in the car."

"Why did you want to know how much money the guy got?" I asked.

"Because now I know he doesn't have a lot of cash, so it won't last him long," said Earl. "This means he'll strike again real soon, maybe in the next day or two."

That made sense to me. This was obviously an example of how using your mind could solve little riddles that might eventually help break a case. Still, could using my mind ever help me receive honor, bravery, and courage? It seemed to be impossible at the moment.

As we got back to the station, Earl said, "Sounds just like the guy we're looking for in all the other robberies."

"Yep, maybe it's him and we'll catch him," I said.

The look on Earl's face seemed to say, "Of course, we will catch him." This was the kind of encouragement I needed. Finally, I saw the possibility that if I could not find honor, bravery, and courage by using my mind, I could at least use every natural ability I had to catch this robber, or at least make Earl proud of me. One very important thing to me is that people in this world would see that I am trying, in fact, to live life right and be a good person. Still, people in society require so much more in order for someone to be perceived as a unique individual.

How did my grandfather do it? How did my father do it? How was it that when their names are mentioned, only respect and admiration follow, rallying every person's undying attention? Was my grandfather above and beyond that of any normal, brave man of his time? Is my father, right now, blessed with courage that only a special few are selected to have from somewhere unknown? And most importantly, was I worthy to even associate my last name with theirs?

Some questions still needed answering; questions that continue on in my mind every day of my life. Where do I continue my search? Where do I even dare to look for such characteristics in myself? Throughout all this, my only priority at the moment was to help Earl solve this case and catch this robber, who had no concern for anyone's safety. He only cared about his selfish desire to get ahead in this world without having to work for it.

As the end of the shift came, Earl asked, "Jack, what are you doing for dinner?"

"I was planning on going back to my apartment and warm up a meal from yesterday," I said.

"No, Jack, you're coming home with me," said Earl.

"If you insist." The truth was I lived by myself, and I did not really have many friends, much less girlfriends, to spend time with. Earl had shared earlier that he was married with two children. I thought it would be kind of neat to be a part of his family for the night. I followed Earl to his home.

We walked to his front door, and his lovely wife said, "Hi, I'm Jenny, Earl's wife."

Then, without a moment's notice, two young boys came whipping out the front door screaming, "Daddy! Daddy!"

I knew these were Earl's two boys he talked so much about that day. Jimmy was four, and James was six. Both of them looked at me with some curiosity, and Earl finally introduced me. "I want you to meet my new partner, Jack Mayfield." I thought it was terrific of him to introduce me as his partner and not his training rookie.

It did not take long for me to feel at home, except I must be honest, jealousy arose as I saw this police detective with a beautiful wife, two wonderful boys, a home in the city, and even a cute inside dog properly named Warrant. This was the kind of life I dreamed of. Even though Earl was a lot older than me, I thought he had it all. I wondered how long it took him to find this happiness. Could I find this happiness with the honor, bravery, and the unobtainable courage I was looking for? I longed for balance and peace in my life.

As we sat down for dinner, Earl asked me, "Jack, what do you think we should do to catch this guy robbing all the liquor stores?"

I was shocked that Earl, a seasoned police detective veteran, would even want my ideas. I said, "Well, I think time's going to be the key. I think we already know what part of town this guy's robbing, and you already know about what time of day it happens, so maybe if we are lucky ... "

"Go on! Go on!" encouraged Earl.

"Well, maybe if we plan to be in an unmarked squad car about 3:30 tomorrow afternoon, somewhere in the area of the liquor stores he's been robbing, maybe, just maybe, we'll run right into him."

Earl liked the idea. He said, "You know, that sounds so simple, it might just work."

I was pumped. Earl not only showed me the ropes as a new police detective, but he had also taken me under his wing as a companion, not to mention saying he thought my idea was a good one. Man, this felt like it was going to put balance in my life! It felt like I had a purpose and a meaning, like I was meant to do something special in this old world. Maybe I did not need reassurance of having the family trait of courage. Maybe time did not permit my search for courage, and I might only find it when I stopped looking for it. I decided that whatever the outcome of things in my life were, surely each and every action would have a purpose.

I left Earl's home and went back to my apartment with another goal. Sure, I wanted to continue my search for the family traits that could justify my claim on the name Mayfield, but I also had a new search in life—the search for a family of my own; a family filled with happiness, companionship, and true love.

I awoke to a new morning, and with that came a new purpose. I wanted to live life to the fullest. I didn't want to pass up any opportunities that might present themselves. These were all new ideas I obtained after seeing how wonderful Earl and his family were. I longed for that same happiness.

As the day went on, I finally made my way down to the police department for another grueling day of fighting crime. As I entered the building, Earl immediately came up to me and said, "Jack, here is a printout of the local liquor stores that the robber has hit." The printout gave us some idea of the areas the robber was working in. "Let's go for a ride," Earl said.

"Sure, Earl. Where to?"

"To the Forty-fifth Avenue liquor store."

"You mean the one that was robbed yesterday?"

"Yep, the one that was robbed yesterday." Earl went on to tell me of his theory, his "sixth sense," that the robber would hit the same liquor store again.

"Why do you feel that way?" I said.

"Because he only got a $100 the first time, and he saw how easy it was with the little old lady."

This made all the sense in the world to me. I guess a veteran police detective thinks of almost everything. In this case at least, it was a good way to see if other cops also had a sixth sense like I have at times.

As Earl and I got in an unmarked squad car, we headed down 5th Street toward the area of the Forty-fifth Avenue liquor store. Out of curiosity, I looked at my watch and noticed it was 3:15 p.m.

Out of nowhere came the police dispatcher on the police radio, "Attention, all units! Attention, all units! An armed robbery just occurred. I repeat, an armed robbery just occurred. It happened at the Forty-fifth Avenue liquor store. The description of the suspect is a black male about 5 foot 9 wearing khaki pants, a white T-shirt, and carrying a pillowcase with a flower print on it."

I thought, *Man, that is a good description!* Later, we found out that the store clerk, who was the same little old lady, did not get as scared this time. Instead, she got mad. She got so frustrated that the same guy robbed her two days in a row that she immediately picked up the phone when the suspect left and called 9-1-1. She gave a super description of the guy.

We were really close to the liquor store now.

"Earl, drive down the alley coming up." I was familiar with this alley from my patrol days. "And come up the back way to the liquor store."

As we went down the alley, this black male about 5 foot 9, wearing khaki pants and a white T-shirt came out of nowhere. He had something in his hands, but I could not see exactly what it was.

I yelled, "That's him! That's him!"

Earl started slowing down the car, and just before the car came to a complete stop, my old patrol days kicked in, and I bailed out of the car and engaged the suspect in a foot chase through the alley.

We ran, and ran, and ran. I yelled to the suspect, "Stop, you moron! Police!" and a few other not so nice phrases, but the suspect kept running.

I could hear Earl yell out loud, "Jack, be careful! He has a gun!"

I must say, I did not really think about that until Earl mentioned it, and this was bad because detectives did not normally wear bulletproof vests like most patrolmen do. I had to take that into consideration as I chased this unpredictable bad guy down the sidewalk, hoping he did not turn around and shoot me. As I started getting closer to the suspect, he cut through someone's backyard and straight into a wooded area. I did the same thing, only now I pulled my gun out because I lost sight of him just for a split second. As I turned around in the woods, I regained my sight of the suspect. He had his back to me, and I yelled at him, "Get down on the ground, or I will end all your problems in life!"

The suspect lay down on the ground. I approached him very cautiously and placed handcuffs on him. Fortunately, I saw him in the woods before he saw me, or else the outcome might have been different. As I started walking the suspect out of the woods back to a populated area, I could hear Earl calling for me. "Jack! Where are you? Jack!"

This made me feel good, because I was cared about. I yelled back, "I'm okay, and I got you a surprise!"

As Earl and I made eye contact, he could see I had the suspect in custody, and he gave me a grin as if to say, "Good job." Let's face it, though, we are both men, and cops at that. You can't expect to get too sentimental.

Earl and I took the suspect back to the police department he and said, "Not bad for your second day as a police detective, huh?" I could only chuckle at that. "What's so funny?" Earl said.

"I took the promotion for police detective so I wouldn't have to do this kind of stuff anymore."

Seeing the humor, Earl said, "Well, at least you got your health."

After all the adventures in my law enforcement career, I still had an empty place inside of me. The search for my family heritage had left me weak and feeling futile in some aspects. I doubted not only my actions in life, but also my being. I wanted the reassurance of being a true Mayfield. I wanted to be somebody who stood out in society as a good and honorable man, with bravery and courage as his allies. I find now, after my long journey, that maybe my hunch about being a plain, normal guy could be the conclusion to my search. Maybe it was my destiny to always search for that elusive, characteristic family trait, courage, that all Mayfields had. Maybe now I could finally rest knowing that there would be no honor, bravery, or family courage to be found, only the search. With all these contemplations every hour of my day, the one thing I longed for more than anything was love and a family of my own. With these things, it could be very possible to replace the family traits that had only left me empty inside.

Chapter Twelve

Capturing Courage

As I have said so very often, the Mayfield men in my family had honor, bravery, and courage above and beyond that of an everyday person. I have not mentioned very many Mayfield women and how the same qualities can be found in their veins as well. The Mayfield men and women are and always will be special.

Grandmother Mayfield must have been some kind of woman. She not only raised four children, but she always took excellent care of Grandfather Mayfield. Despite the difficulties Grandfather dealt with in his time— a time of great burdens to bear—he worked all the way up into his early seventies to provide for his family in any way he could.

I learned through stories that Grandfather worked one job, then came home, ate, then went back out to go to his second job at night. During the Depression, money was very hard to come by for families. For my grandfather, this saying was most definitely true: Behind every good man, there is a good woman.

I can testify that my grandmother lived up to the definition of a "good woman." Although I only knew her for a short time, the stories of her spoke so honestly about her that I can only picture her as being a special person in my grandfather's life. Certainly, Grandfather Mayfield had strong family values, and I believe Grandmother did, too. After all, she had to keep things running smoothly at home, and she and Grandfather had little time together while he worked two jobs. I do believe that Grandmother gave Grandfather the peace and stability that he needed in order to fulfill his strong family beliefs. Grandmother must have given Grandfather strength during dire times.

I would imagine Grandmother had to be very resilient and resourceful to make ends meet, and for the house to run smoothly. Her specialty was being the tough one in the family, and the only one who could handle Grandfather Mayfield. That surely says something about Grandmother, because Grandfather was a tough guy. Grandmother Mayfield, a sweet, little lady would back Grandfather, the tough guy, into a corner to make her point or to tell him what he aught *not* to do.

Grandfather Mayfield, I was told, could only put up his hands and say, "Now, Mamie. Now, Mamie." That was what my grandfather called my grandmother. I reckon if my grandmother was able to stand up to my grandfather, then she too must have had the kind of personality that said, "Hello, world. I will take you on anytime, anywhere." She truly must have been some kind of woman.

I cannot leave out another important woman bearing the Mayfield name. My mother is undoubtedly one of the toughest women alive. She came from a rural area in Georgia, and was raised picking cotton at six-years-old, trying her best to fill up one five-gallon bucket before the day ended. If she accomplished this, she would receive her dollar and fifty cents for the whole long day's worth of work. She did not mind, though, because her brothers and sister were right there in the fields with her. She always told me that her childhood did not have much joy or happiness, because there was no time for fun and games. There was only work. Despite being a warrior as a child, she grew into the most elegant lady I have ever known in my life. I used to describe her to my friends as being "proper." She had all the dignity and manners required to dine with the elaborate upper-echelon people in society. Still, she remained down to earth, and cared very much for people.

Every so often, I can see how my father got "hooked" the first time he met her, but she also found my father to be an undiscovered treasure.

My father, being raised the way he was, had the Mayfield mentality that sometimes got in the way of showing his sensitive side. Mother found a way to chisel away the stone around my dad's heart, and it spoke highly of her ability to love and understand him. Inside that tough, rugged man, my mother knew of the sensitive and caring man my father could be; a man who wanted only good things for his entire family. Yes, he too had to work under extremely tough conditions. Like his father, he had more than one job, and his attitude mirrored Grandfather's strong family ethics. My father only wanted to provide for his family the best he could. The strong family ethic turns out to be a common characteristic along with the honor, bravery, and courage that most Mayfields possess.

Albeit my personal search for these things, I wondered if I would be fortunate enough to ever find a good woman. It appeared that most good men were lucky enough if they had a good woman by their sides. Unlike other Mayfields in the family, I had yet to find what was so alluring about the Mayfield men that they attracted such wonderful women.

It could be an attraction to those qualities I believed were hiding from me. I believe they find security and comfort, as well as dedication and honesty, in knowing their Mayfield men have honor, bravery, and beyond average courage. Knowing they have chosen a man of distinction may be what gives them peace of mind in this world at any given time, in any given situation.

Never feeling worthy of the Mayfield name, I never really looked for true love in my life. I had the important search to concentrate on. At least, I thought my personal search for my family heritage and inherited traits would mean something in this world, but after years of searching to no avail, I realized my life was being lived in vain and selfish, wonton admiration; that need for acceptance in society as being a true Mayfield. All I need to be was myself, even if that meant a plain, normal guy who was just like everybody else. This seemed only logical to me and my outlook in life.

Somehow, within my law enforcement career, I was always in the company of the opposite sex. I went on dates. I went out to eat. I went to movies, but none of the women were able to replace the search going on within me; replace the empty questions that remained inside of me. After many disappointing relationships, I gave up my search for my family honor and courage.

After seeing Earl's life both as a detective and a family man, I was becoming willing to give up my search for that special someone who could only be heaven-sent. I wanted to give up my search for true love.

You could ask me, "How could I give up my relentless pursuit?" The answer was simple. I was tired. Tired of rejections. Tired of pursuing my heritage. Tired of trying to be a Mayfield man. I found it so difficult to believe that a family's reputation could be so hard to possess. It was time for everything to be natural and right in front of me. It was time for reality, but I had only more trials and tribulations to deal with.

One day, my boss assigned me to investigate an aggravated assault case that had occurred the previous night. A man by the name of Glenn Rogers was hit on the head with a broken beer bottle. The case did not amount to much, however, I did have to go to the local hospital to check on the victim and see the extent of his injuries.

This was a first, going to the hospital to determine someone else's injuries instead of my own. Kind of ironic, if you ask me. As I arrived at the hospital, I took the elevator to the Glen Rogers' floor. Before I went inside his room, I knocked first, strictly for professional reasons, and then I introduced myself. "Hello, I'm Detective Mayfield with the police department here in town." Rogers must have been on some pain medicine or something, because he looked like a deer caught in headlights. Starting a normal conversation, I asked, "Do you know who hit you?"

Surprisingly, Mr. Rogers said, "Yeah, it was my brother."

"Your brother?" I said with a puzzled look on my face.

"Yep, my brother," said Rogers.

"Why did your brother hit you with a beer bottle?" I asked.

"Maybe because I stole his girlfriend."

"Yeah, I guess that would do it."

Glenn Rogers laughed.

There came a shy little knock at the door, and Glenn Rogers said, "Come in."

There, before my mesmerized eyes, stood an angel. It was Glenn Rogers' nurse. She *was* beautiful. She had lovely dark brown hair, brown eyes, and a smooth-looking olive complexion. I stared at her endlessly.

"Time for your medicine, Mr. Rogers," she said, barely even noticing me.

I knew I had to do something right then. For the first time in my Mayfield life, I felt all tangled up. It was not the so-called sixth sense or the boldness I felt when going after an armed robber. This new feeling made my knees turn to rubber. I gathered what little bit of confidence I had and said, "Excuse me, nurse. How bad is Mr. Rogers' injury?" This question, I hoped, would get this angel to notice me without my being so obvious. I hoped she could not see my emotional turmoil.

She replied with the softest-spoken voice I have ever heard. "He has a concussion, but he should be going home soon."

As she started to leave, I reached deep down to locate some Mayfield courage and charm. Stuttering, I asked, "Wa ... What's your name?"

"Elizabeth, Elizabeth Robinson," she said as she turned back around, an illuminating smile angelically appearing on her face.

"Well, Miss Elizabeth Robinson, my name is Jack, and I would love to take you out to eat tonight if you have no prior plans."

"I would love to," said Elizabeth, "only I do have a prior engagement."

"Oh," I said. Time stopped for a moment. The thought of falling in love had gone by the wayside. Something came over me as I snapped back into my body, but before I realized it, I asked, "Well, if tonight's a bad time, how about tomorrow night?"

She did not answer right away. I thought, *Maybe she was concerned with my profession, or maybe I wasn't up to her standards.* Whatever the reason, she finally replied, "Okay, here's my number. Call me tomorrow afternoon, and we'll see what happens."

She then left the room as a petal falls from a rose, and I had this exciting feeling that something special had just happened. I stared at the door, hoping Elizabeth would come back. Reality came back when I heard Glenn Rogers' clouded sense of humor. "Damn, I need to be a policeman." Obviously, Glen Rogers saw what went on between Elizabeth and me.

But wait, "Tomorrow." I thought, *What do I wear? What do I say? What do I do?* Surely my father and Grandfather Mayfield never acted like this when trying to obtain true love. Or did they?

I went straight home from work that night while the name Elizabeth ran in my mind over and over. Just picturing her entering the room, and the way she gave Rogers his medicine, and how her just being there made me feel as if the world had just come to a complete stop. At that very moment, she made me feel as though my entire life was not wasted away in vain. She gave me hope; hope that I could still find a balance in life; hope that I could continue my search for my family traits; hope that she might truly be sent from heaven above, of us going through this world, living and dreaming of only wonderful things to come. I must say, these were a lot of things to swallow at one time, but for a man who has beaten the odds on more than several occasions, I thought, "*What the hell?*"

As the day of the big first date came, I spent much time washing my car, ironing my clothes, and rehearsing my lines to impress Miss Elizabeth Robinson. Before I knew it, it was time to pick her up. I called her first thing that morning, and she agreed to go to a movie, and then maybe out to eat. As I pulled up into her driveway, I felt my knees shaking a bit. I tried to summon up courage. *Come on, Jack! You've run down an armed robber with a gun. You've fallen through the ceiling of the police department. You even jumped into an out-of-control moving car. Surely you can go to the door and ring the doorbell.*

Finally, I convinced myself. I made my way to her front porch, and just as I went to ring the doorbell, the door opened. Elizabeth stood there with this big smile on her face, and she said, "Are you ready to go?"

"Yeah," was all I could muster up. I wondered if Elizabeth could see right through me. The tough police training never prepared me for this night, or what was to come next.

We were driving to the movies, and as luck would have it, we ended up behind a vehicle stopped in the middle of the turn lane. We waited patiently behind the vehicle, assuming car trouble was the culprit. Then we noticed the passenger of the vehicle exit out the passenger's side door. He started walking away from the car. Unexpectedly, the driver of the vehicle exited out of the driver's side, and started yelling at the passenger to get back in the vehicle. When the passenger refused to acknowledge the driver, he began following the passenger, leaving the car parked in the middle of the turn lane and blocking not just us, but several other cars waiting to turn.

As a police detective and so-called veteran policeman, I had learned by now not to get involved in things when off duty. In this case, I believed that if I did not do something immediately, we would miss the movie. On the other hand, Elizabeth might think badly of me.

Politely, I exited the car. I caught up with the driver and said, "Please move your car."

The driver decided to give me the middle finger. I then proceeded to produce my gold detective badge and asked him again, using choice words this time. "Move your car, idiot, or I'll have it towed." You guessed it, the driver saw it my way.

Still, I wondered what Elizabeth was thinking at this point on our first date. As I got back in the car, I asked Elizabeth. "You're used to this kind of excitement, right?"

She quietly said, "Not at all, but I definitely could stand a little excitement in my life." Then she smiled, and off we went to the movies.

After the movie ended, I asked Elizabeth, "Do you want to go get something to eat?"

"Sure, that sounds great," she said.

We went to the Old Ranch restaurant, famous for good ole southern cooking and hospitality. When Elizabeth and I ordered our food, she commented, "How nice is our waitress and this environment?"

"I agree."

Seated right next to us was a man and woman also having dinner. We noticed them because, unfortunately, they were engaged in an argument. Their voices started to get louder and louder. Elizabeth asked, "Are you going to say something?"

I could hear the concern in Elizabeth's voice, but I told her, "Well, it's not really my place, unless someone asks me to help."

Just as I said that, the manager of the restaurant came out to where the loud couple was sitting. I heard the manager ask the couple politely, "Could you please keep it down? If there's anything I could get you ... "

The man started saying vulgar words and using profanity, and the woman became irate.

Elizabeth looked at me, concerned. She obviously wanted me to do something. On that cue, I gracefully got up from my table and asked the manager, "Is everything okay?"

Before the manager could say anything, the man asked, "What business is it of yours, dumbass?"

First of all, I did not like the tone in the guy's voice. Second, I did not really like being called a dumbass. Before I knew it, the Mayfield blood started boiling inside me, and I leaned over and quietly told the confused man, "Look, bonehead, I'm a cop, and if you want to have a new pair of cufflinks, I have some that will definitely fit you perfectly. Now, either get up and leave the restaurant, or you sit there like you have some sense and finish your meal."

The would-be tough guy knew I was not bluffing, so he and his woman decided to leave without any further problems.

I sat back down at the table and finished my meal with beautiful Elizabeth Robinson sitting next to me. I asked Elizabeth, "How do you feel about what just happened, and about the night in general?"

She said, "I guess you can never really stop being a cop once you become one." This made sense to me, and really, it made me feel good. I finally found someone other than a cop who could relate to me, and understand what was important to me.

As the night ended, I took Elizabeth back to her home and asked her, "Do you think you would like to go out again sometime?"

"I would love to," she said.

This made my night! I went straight home and fell asleep dreaming of the first date that I had with Elizabeth Robinson.

As the days went by, I was able to see Elizabeth more and more. It was like we hit it off right from the beginning. She was a good listener, and boy let me tell you, I really liked to talk. It was like we were meant to be together. We did lunches, movies, and walks in the park, and we made time for each other. Basically, I guess you could say we were falling in love. This must have been what it was, because I had never had this feeling inside for another woman before. I could not wait to see Elizabeth each time.

I must say, though, the relationship took my focus away from my job. I took some time off to spend with Elizabeth. In my mind, this was more important than my job or my search for those family traits I so desperately sought.

Speaking of which, I wondered if my personal search would continue now that I found something more important to me. Elizabeth was becoming my every breath. I could not stop thinking of her every waking hour of the day. This experience became so strong that it began to change my outlook on life. I started thinking differently from the way I did before I met Elizabeth. At one time in my law enforcement career, I feared nothing. I did not worry about getting shot, stabbed, or injured in any way. Now, to take a chance on anything that might keep me from being in this tender-loving relationship with Elizabeth brought a kind of fear.

It seemed like the other detectives, as well as the other sworn officers, noticed I was not the same aggressive, carefree man that the old Jack Mayfield used to be. I asked myself, *Is that a bad thing?* I mean, wanting to spend every chance I got with the woman of my dreams, whom I now had deep and true feelings for—did that make me less of a man? Did this take away any honor, bravery, and courage I might have? I decided to talk with Elizabeth and see how she felt about everything.

On our next date, we got a chance to talk without distractions. I began by saying, "Elizabeth, I want to discuss something with you."

"Okay, go ahead," she said.

"It's about the Mayfield men who have come before me, the family name and the family traits. The Mayfield men have always stood out above ordinary men. I have searched for years to find the same true honor, bravery, and courage my father and grandfather possessed. For some reason, I never felt like those traits had been passed on to me. I thought that if I had inherited those traits, then peace and a balance would come into my life. No matter how much I looked, and no matter how much I tried, never did I believe those characteristics were passed on to me. I felt I was not deserving of carrying the Mayfield name. Not much has seemed important to me other than law enforcement. Police work, I thought, might bring out those family traits, but the reputation I got was that of a crazy cowboy. I believed that if I got the bad guys and put them away, this would make me eligible to carry the Mayfield name. Basically, I don't feel deserving of the Mayfield name." I concluded, "It seems to me that the Mayfield traits must be a requirement in order to stand out from an everyday person. I think it's turned out that I'm just a plain ole everyday person, and there's nothing special about me. I still feel empty in that regard."

Elizabeth listened intently, and her facial expression showed concern. She said, "Jack, I understand about your personal search in life, and I understand about your feeling empty," she continued, "but Jack, you have to be yourself. Any inner honor, bravery, or family courage you have will come out when it's time." I did not really understand what Elizabeth meant by that, but just knowing she was okay with what I was dealing with inside gave me peace of mind.

As the months went by, I began to realize that I wanted to spend the rest of my life with Elizabeth. I bought a ring, then worked up the nerve one afternoon and went to the hospital where I first met Elizabeth. I saw her at the nurse's station on the floor she worked, and I went to her and said, "Hello, Elizabeth. Is there somewhere we can talk privately?"

Elizabeth seemed surprised to see me at her work, and later she told me how nervous she felt when I asked her to go to a private location in the hospital. She said, "Sure, Jack. Let me clock out for my break, and we can go to the nurse's lounge." I watched while Elizabeth clocked out, and then she led me to the nurse's lounge. As we entered the lounge, I was relieved to see that no one else was in the room. Elizabeth turned to me and said, "What's wrong? Did I do something wrong?"

"No, sweetheart. That's just it," I said. "You've done everything right." I got on one knee, held up the ring to her, and said, "Elizabeth Elaine Robinson, will you marry me?"

Tears welled up in her eyes as she replied, "Yes, I would love to marry you, Jack."

She put on the ring, and after a long sentimental hug, and many—I mean, many—kisses, I told Elizabeth, "I love you. Now, get back to work." As I left the hospital, I can honestly say I felt like a new man, like the entire world was at my beck and call. I was the happiest I had ever been in my entire life. Could this be it? Was I now a good man? I must be, because the saying goes: Behind every good man, there is a good woman. And let me tell you, there was a good woman in Elizabeth.

Planning the wedding took several weeks, and it was just too long for me. I wanted to be Elizabeth's husband as soon as possible. Finally, the big day came, and I stood next to the woman I truly loved, with my father as my best man, while my mother and her family looked on. I said my vows and watched as she said hers, and then it happened. We were pronounced husband and wife. The years of searching for true love had finally ended. Elizabeth was now my life, and I was hers. We went on a brief honeymoon, and then back to the house I had recently bought.

Before I knew it, I was back working as a police detective, and she continued in her nursing profession. We were happy. The happiness seemed endless, but after a year or two, I realized something. I realized that my search for true love had ended; however, my search for the Mayfield honor, bravery, and courage still continued. Was I now a normal man doing what all normal men do? I worked, came home, took care of the yard and the house, and paid bills. This was my new focus instead of the personal family traits that I seemed to be lacking.

As more time went by, I became more depressed. Elizabeth started noticing the changes in me. She said, "Jack, you mean so much to me. Please stop searching for the family traits, because you already have them."

Still, until I could see the traits for myself, I would always have doubts in my heart; doubts that I was deserving of the Mayfield name; doubt that I was a true man; doubt that I would be able to go through this world taking on any and everything that came my way. The more I thought about it, the more depressed I became.

Elizabeth finally called my father and said, "Jack seems troubled. It's affecting our marriage."

My father, being the good Mayfield man he was, called me and asked me to come over to his house to spend some time with him. I agreed, and the first Saturday in April became the most important day for me.

After I arrived, we sat down, and my father said, "Jack, what's troubling you?"

"Dad, I feel it's so important for me to be as brave and honorable as you and Grandfather Mayfield. It's important for me to find courage within my own self, and to take on any trials and tribulations this world brings my way, but most of all, I need to know I am a man, a Mayfield man, deserving of the prestigious name and reputation that goes with it."

My father listened to my every want, wish, and desire. He simply said, "Boy," (which is the name my father has always called me; never Jack, only Boy.) "Boy, a true man is a complex creature with many good points as well as faults that makes up his ... my way of describing a man is a person who has complete control over all his emotions and actions. A man is one in control of his anger, sadness, excitement, love and fear. A man is much more than anything you could ever describe, but to me, a man is someone who takes responsibility in life and accepts his role as being a provider and a caretaker, and if need be, like in your profession, an enforcer; someone to bring peace to any situation, someone who has patience and understanding, and someone who also has wisdom." This, coming from my father, really hit home. We concluded our conversation, and as I left his house, he said one more thing to me. "Boy, no matter what you think, you've always been a Mayfield, and you've always been a son I've been proud of."

My father smiled at me, and at that moment, I realized that whether or not I have the inherited honor, bravery, or courage my father and grandfather had, I could at least be proud of the fact that I was the offspring of honor, bravery, and courage. This gave me some ease.

I went home and spent the rest of the weekend with my loving wife, Elizabeth. As Monday came, I got ready for work, and told Elizabeth that I loved her very much. Elizabeth had followed me outside, and before I got to the car, she said, "I need to tell you something," a huge smile on her face.

Just then, I heard the dispatcher say over the police radio, "All units! All units! Be advised a semi-truck and trailer has overturned near the exit ramp of mile marker 150." It just so happened Elizabeth and I lived within two blocks of the interstate and of mile marker 150. The dispatcher then said over the police radio, "All units! All units! The driver of the truck is trapped in the cab of the overturned truck, and the truck is leaking fuel." Well, after hearing this, the Mayfield blood began to tell me to go and do something. My mind told me that I was a detective, and that patrol officers could handle it, but my heart and inner Mayfield feelings were telling me I was probably closer than anyone else who could help, and that maybe I was the guy's only chance.

As I jumped into my car, Elizabeth said in a frightened voice, "Jack, I have to tell you something really important."

"Can it wait?"

She saw me put the car in gear, and knowing how aggressive I could be, she said quickly, "You're going to be a daddy." She wanted me to know for the fear of something bad to come.

I looked at her with shock at first; then I smiled and said, "That's great news, sweetie! I'll be home later and we'll celebrate."

Elizabeth watched as I sped out of the driveway and proceeded as fast as I could to the accident only two blocks away. On my way to the scene, I could only think of how wonderful it was going to be to become a father. I was so proud. As I reached the interstate ramp, I could see the overturned semi-truck and trailer. I could also see fuel leaking very fast from the fuel tank. I told the dispatcher, "Detective Mayfield on the scene. Dispatch, send me some help! There's leaking gas."

I got out of my vehicle and climbed up to see inside the cab. I noticed a white male lying unconscious, his face away from me, with blood in several places that must have been from the accident. I tried with all my might to get the cab door open, but to no avail. It just would not move. The windshield was blocked by debris and unmovable objects. The only way to get to the injured driver was through the cab door window that was not big enough for any adult to fit through.

I thought to myself, *Think, Jack, think!* I ended up trying to wedge myself through the cab door window, and with lady luck on my side, I was able to fit through. When I finally got inside the cab, I tried to get the injured driver to wake up. I said to him, "Come on! Come on! We have to get out of here. The truck is leaking fuel."

The man made no movement at first, then as he came to some, he said, "I think my leg is broken." I saw where his leg was pinned under the passenger side seat. It looked rather painful, wedged in between the metal braces. I said, "Sir, just stay calm." I tried to see if I could free his leg, but as I tried, it only sent the injured driver into screams of agony. The man was covered in blood, and his leg was definitely broken. He could not move.

Suddenly, my mind thought of the worst thing imaginable. *Jack, you're going to be a father, and the truck is going to catch on fire at any time. There is leaking fuel, and there's no way you can get the man and yourself out of here. Leave, Jack. Just get out of here.*

Yes, it was true. I felt something very different from before. I felt real fear. I had a lot to loose, and I wondered if I would ever see my wife and unborn child. I was truly scared, and I realized that at any minute, the truck was going to explode into flames, and the injured driver and I would undoubtedly meet our fates. Fear showed in the driver's eyes, and as I tried one more time to free his leg so that we could go out through the cab door window, he said to me, "It's okay, save yourself."

Then it happened again, something inside of me spoke up. I came to the conclusion that fear was not part of this equation, that if it was the truck driver's fate to be sealed in this truck, it would be my fate to die trying to save him. I could not leave; I could not desert someone in need. I stood to lose everything in life that meant the world to me, but to leave would mean being that person I hated the most in life—the one who quits.

For the first time in my life, I realized something. I realized that the inner voice in my heart was my Mayfield blood telling me how to live my life. "I am a man," it said. "I am a Mayfield man, and I will stay until the end."

I started smelling the fuel leaking from the truck. The smell became stronger and stronger, and I asked the injured driver, "What is your name?"

He replied, "Roy. Roy Collins."

I said, "Roy Collins, I am Detective Mayfield, and I just learned that I am going to be a daddy. Don't you worry; the Lord will take care of everything."

Just then, I heard the faint sound of fire trucks and other emergency response units in the distance. As the sirens got closer, I knew we were running out of time, but I also knew, out of everything I had been through, that I had always beaten the odds. I knew then that I could beat them one more time.

Roy looked at me and said, "Thank you for not leaving me."

Just then the "jaws of life" cranked up, and I heard voices saying, "Hang tight. We'll get you out of there."

The jaws of life was what the fire department used to cut trapped people out of vehicles when there were no other options. As the cab side door was cut off, I knew I could get out right then, but I stayed until the ambulance ENT brought a stretcher, and the fire units were able to free Mr. Collins' leg from beneath the seat. As Mr. Collins was lifted out of the cab of the overturned truck, I helped carry him to a nearby waiting ambulance. Right after that, the truck went up in flames, and it was apparent to me that the fuel finally had ignited somehow. It also was apparent that, once again, I had beaten the odds.

As the ambulance drove off with Mr. Collins inside, I watched the fire department extinguish the flames from the truck and trailer. I realized I was completely covered in blood and broken glass. A patrol supervisor at the scene asked if I was injured or needed any medical assistance, but I told him, "No, thank you. I just want to go home and see my wife."

I left the scene of the accident and drove the two blocks back to my house. Three hours had passed when I finally pulled into the driveway of my home. I saw Elizabeth waiting for me on the porch with teary eyes. As I got out of my vehicle and started walking toward her, she rushed right off the porch and grabbed me. She said, "Oh, Jack, I love you so much! You mean everything to me."

Suddenly, Elizabeth noticed the blood and broken glass on me and started to get worried. I said, "Honey, I'm fine. I've never been better."

Elizabeth asked, "What do you mean?"

"Elizabeth," I said, "I might not be the smartest guy in the world, and I know I'm not the best looking guy in the world, but there is no doubt in my mind that I am the luckiest guy in the world."

Elizabeth thought I was referring to my latest law enforcement adventure involving the overturned truck and trailer, but what I really meant was being married to a wonderful, loving and caring wife, having a wonderful family, and now, with the most wonderful news any man could ever receive, "You're going to be a father."

Finally, I understood. I understood my place in this world, and I understood my life in society. I knew that being a man, a good Mayfield man, did not mean you had to show you were brave or honorable. I realized that most courageous and brave men never see themselves as being so. I also realized that just going through this old world doing what is right, like working, settling down, getting married, and raising a family, was what one needed to be a man. True enough, goodness would be shown through ones actions, but in my case, goodness came from just living life to the fullest with my most beautiful wife, who is undoubtedly my true soul mate, and with the birth of our first child, who turned out to be the cutest, most precious baby girl in the whole world. I now understand what is honorable and brave.

The search finally ended. I have found my inherited courage.